HURON COUNTY LIBRARY

3 6492 00517101 9

D1622165

SPECIAL MESSAGE TO READERS

This book is published under the auspices of

THE ULVERSCROFT FOUNDATION

(registered charity No. 264873 UK)

Established in 1972 to provide funds for research, diagnosis and treatment of eye diseases. Examples of contributions made are: —

A Children's Assessment Unit at
Moorfield's Hospital, London.

•

Twin operating theatres at the
Western Ophthalmic Hospital, London.

•

A Chair of Ophthalmology at the
Royal Australian College of Ophthalmologists.

•

The Ulverscroft Children's Eye Unit at the
Great Ormond Street Hospital For Sick Children,
London.

You can help further the work of the Foundation by making a donation or leaving a legacy. Every contribution, no matter how small, is received with gratitude. Please write for details to:

THE ULVERSCROFT FOUNDATION,
The Green, Bradgate Road, Anstey,
Leicester LE7 7FU, England.
Telephone: (0116) 236 4325

In Australia write to:
THE ULVERSCROFT FOUNDATION,
c/o The Royal Australian and New Zealand
College of Ophthalmologists,
94-98 Chalmers Street, Surry Hills,
N.S.W. 2010, Australia

SHADOW OF THE FLAME

When zoology student Lisa Ryding first meets wildlife film-maker Guy Barrington at Oxford University, she is prepared to follow him to the ends of the earth. But a secret too tragic for Guy to reveal makes this impossible. Five years later, they are thrown together on a remote game reserve in Zambia by their mutual passion to save the elephant from extinction. When Guy is bitten by a snake and nearly dies, Lisa realises that nothing will ever change her love for him and her only salvation will be to never see him again.

Books by Sheila Belshaw
in the Linford Romance Library:

THE NIGHTINGALE WILL SING
DIAMONDS OF THE SUN
SAVAGE PARADISE

SHEILA BELSHAW

SHADOW OF THE FLAME

Complete and Unabridged

LINFORD
Leicester

First published in Great Britain in 2004

First Linford Edition
published 2005

Copyright © 2004 by Sheila Belshaw
All rights reserved

British Library CIP Data

Belshaw, Sheila
    Shadow of the flame.—Large print ed.—
    Linford romance library
    1. Love stories
    2. Large type books
    I. Title
    823.9'14 [F]

    ISBN 1–84395–896–1

Published by
F. A. Thorpe (Publishing)
Anstey, Leicestershire

Set by Words & Graphics Ltd.
Anstey, Leicestershire
Printed and bound in Great Britain by
T. J. International Ltd., Padstow, Cornwall

This book is printed on acid-free paper

1

At the edge of her vision Lisa caught a sudden movement — a crouched figure in the empty shimmering distance. With a quick twist of her wrist she adjusted the lenses of her binoculars and focused on the figure.

Like the sudden onrush of a tidal wave in a calm sea, she felt a surge that began in her stomach and ended somewhere in her throat.

No, she told herself. It couldn't be him. It couldn't be anyone she knew. Not in the middle of Africa, in an almost inaccessible Zambian game reserve . . .

The two pregnant elephant cows she'd been tracking all day emerged from the trees on the left of the lagoon, heading for the river. She re-adjusted her binoculars. For a few moments she stood still, mesmerised by their majesty.

But there was that movement again. Abandoning the elephant cows, Lisa swivelled round and focused on the north bank of the lagoon.

The distant figure was standing up now. There was something agonisingly familiar about his stance, his shape, the very way he held the camera.

She steadied the binoculars.

He was tall and lean. His hair, caught by the setting sun, was golden and he was holding a large camera.

This was a wildlife photographer's paradise but it was way off the tourist track. He must be someone from the film unit the Wildlife people in Lusaka had told her was in the vicinity of her camp. Well, she had no intention of getting mixed up with those people, so it was unlikely she would ever meet him.

She turned away, angry with herself for reacting so violently to the sight of a mere stranger.

But was he a stranger?

They all looked the same in the bush,

with their khaki shorts and shirts and knee-high socks, didn't they?

A breeze rustled through the leaves of the acacia trees, giving her a blissful moment of relief from the heat. The sun was like a balloon blown up to its limit and lit by a flame from within, plunging through the layer of dust suspended above the parched red earth. Soon it would be gone and darkness would descend.

Lisa shivered. The elephants had disappeared beyond the trees, the smell of their dust drifting towards her nostrils. Hurrying to her Land Rover, she stacked her binoculars and cameras into the brand new four-by-four, grudgingly acknowledging that without at last agreeing to spend some of the fortune her father had left her, she could never have afforded any of this obscenely expensive equipment.

She turned for one last look at the man at the edge of the lagoon. In spite of the fading light he was still engrossed in his photography.

She took a long, deep breath, then drove off through the trees, her heart hammering like the drumbeats wafting on the wind from the village downstream.

★ ★ ★

A tent in the middle of a game reserve was probably the noisiest place anyone could choose to spend the night. When darkness fell it seemed to signal the go-ahead for every animal within a hundred miles to communicate with its friends. It would take a few more nights to acclimatise to the unfamiliar sounds, but Lisa knew that this was not the only reason for her inability to sleep.

When the first light of dawn filtered through the canvas she was still wide-awake. Through the patch of gauze above her bed, she watched the swift transition of the sky from grey to pale blue. Suddenly, above the chorus of early morning grunts, snorts and songs, she heard the sound of an aircraft engine.

Quickly she wriggled out of her sleeping bag. She unzipped the front of the tent just as a helicopter lurched low over her camp. Like a giant dragonfly it hovered above her head, the draft from its whirring blades almost ripping the T-shirt from her body.

'Of all the cheek!' she muttered, holding her hands to her ears.

As she glanced up, the machine dipped audaciously towards her tent. A golden head leaned over. She saw the man's startled look, saw a grin spread over his face as he turned to the pilot. It wasn't her idea of a friendly grin, more one of triumph, she thought as the aircraft turned and clattered over the canopy of trees.

Flopping down on to her three-legged stool Lisa sank her head in her hands.

He was the same man she'd seen yesterday. The man with the camera.

Guy Barrington?

It was an alarming thought, and she dismissed it instantly, as she always did when memories of Guy threatened to disrupt her life.

The last time she'd seen Guy was over five years ago at Oxford University. According to media reports, he made all his wildlife films in South America. So how could it be him?

She would never have agreed to do this research for Keep Elephants Alive if she'd known that Guy Barrington was within a thousand miles of her research territory.

A fish-eagle swooped over her camp, circled once, then cried out on its journey towards the sun. Its plaintive song was music to her ears, part of the sound of the Africa she had grown to love, and for a moment she was distracted.

'Breakfast, Lisa?' Enoch said, using one of the ten English words he knew. Smiling broadly he handed her a golden pawpaw he'd brought from his garden in the nearby village where he lived with his family.

Lisa had never tasted anything so

delicious, and insisted that Enoch have the other half. With breakfast complete, she moved to the small wooden table she'd erected in the shade of the ebony tree that dominated her temporary home. Determined to make a start on her report for Keep Elephants Alive, she opened her laptop and typed **Introduction.**

But that was as far as she got.

It was hopeless. Not only was her mind swamped with memories of Guy, but she found there was far too much to assimilate so soon. It would be better to write the introduction after she'd had a few more days to marshal her thoughts. If only she had someone with whom to analyse her findings. Enoch's local knowledge was vast, but a scientific discussion with her amiable game ranger would be impossible until he had learned more English, or she had studied the local language.

As she packed away her laptop she saw a plume of dust snake towards her camp. Moments later an old battered

Land Rover rattled into the clearing. A slight, olive-skinned girl, about her own age, with short black hair cut in a bouncy bob approached, her mosquito boots throwing up little puffs of dust.

'Hi! I hope I am not intruding,' the girl said, in what to Lisa's ears sounded like a Spanish accent.

'Hello,' Lisa said, taking in the neat figure in cropped khaki shorts. 'I'm about to have a mug of coffee. Would you like one?' she asked, as one did in the bush, even to strangers.

'Sure,' the girl said. Her dark, slanting eyes surveyed Lisa's primitive camp. 'We heard you were on your own so I have come to ask you to join us at Hippo Camp tomorrow night, when Tony and Guy get back from Lusaka with the week's supplies.'

Lisa stared speechlessly at her visitor. *Guy?*

So I was right, she thought, steadying herself against the table.

The girl took a step towards Lisa. 'Please come,' she said. 'It will only be

Guy and me and Tony. Tony is our scriptwriter. A real honey. And oh yes, I nearly forgot the new zoologist. Guy is picking her up tomorrow from the airport.'

To refuse such an invitation in the bush would be the height of bad manners. 'Thank you,' Lisa said, trying to appear as outwardly calm as she could while inside every nerve end was on edge. 'I'd love to come.' She handed her visitor a mug of steaming coffee. 'Were those your colleagues I saw in the helicopter early this morning?' she asked, in spite of being quite certain now that they were.

'Yes. It is such a noisy machine, is it not?' the girl answered in the rather quaint, carefully articulated English of a foreigner. 'But it is the only one available around here. Guy hires it for aerial shots and getting supplies from Lusaka. And of course for sending off film to London for processing — '

She clasped her hands together. 'Oh! I am so sorry! I have not introduced myself. I am Iliana de la Rica Alvarez. What is your name?'

'Lisa. Lisa Ryding. I'm a zoologist.'

'Yes, I know. They warned us you would be coming here — '

'Warned you? Who are *they*?'

'The Wildlife Society in Lusaka. They told us Keep Elephants Alive were sending a zoologist to this area. They told us there are more elephants around here than anywhere else in Zambia, so Guy didn't think you would disturb our shoot — '

Suddenly Lisa had to be certain.

'Guy?'

She had only ever known one person called Guy.

'You must have heard of Guy Barrington,' Iliana said, drawing in her breath as though she was inhaling the aroma of a perfumed flower. 'His films are — how do you say? — the Rolls Royces of wildlife films. He is the most . . . *fantastic* cameraman.'

Lisa struggled to keep her hands from shaking. She had watched with tears in her eyes every heart-rending moment of every film he had made in the Amazon River Basin. Films that were always touched with the pathos of animals in jeopardy.

'Yes,' she said. 'I know who you mean. I saw *Conflict*. The one about the endangered jaguars . . . '

Iliana gave Lisa a thoughtful look.

'Oh, really,' she said. 'Well, the World Wildlife Fund commissioned him to make this new film about man's influence on the survival of the elephant. Hey, did I say something wrong? You are very pale. Are you okay?'

'Yes. I'm fine,' Lisa said. 'It's just . . . well, it's just that I get very upset about the way the numbers of elephant have dwindled.'

Iliana's eyes lit up. 'Sure! And that is exactly why Guy wants to show the people who still buy ivory what harm they are doing. The film is being made for television, to coincide with a world-wide campaign. It will also aim to convince the governments of African countries . . . '

But Lisa wasn't listening. She'd been right yesterday. She should have known that no one else stood the way Guy Barrington did, with that strong yet fluid line to his body. That no other man she knew had such golden hair.

She wanted to bombard Iliana with questions, but how could she without betraying her past association with Guy? Iliana was probably his current girlfriend, although recently she'd seen his photograph in The Times, standing next to a girl with frizzy blonde hair, taken at the Wildlife Film Awards ceremony, a different one from the curvaceous female in tow at a previous television interview. She remembered how the sight of this blonde siren clinging to Guy had made her crumple the newspaper and hurl it into the bin.

'You said he was bringing back a new zoologist,' Lisa said, trying not to sound too interested. 'What happened to the old one?' The zoology world was small.

It might even be someone she knew.

Iliana laughed. 'Ginny? Oh, it is a long story. I knew she would never stay. I knew it would never work having her out here, roughing it. She may be a zoologist on paper, but Ginny was useless from the start, and quite . . . unbalanced, I think is the English word.'

Lisa remembered what perfection Guy had always demanded. 'Then why did she come here if she was so useless?'

With the toe of her shoe Iliana drew a circle in the dust, then with her heel she dug a vicious line through it. She paused, then looked up at Lisa. 'Because she wanted Guy. And he was sorry for her. The big soft fool.'

Lisa cleared her throat. 'And what will she do now?'

'Go back to her exciting life in London, I reckon. Africa is quite different from South America, which Ginny loved. But I suppose it sounded glamorous — being on safari in Africa.

With Guy Barrington.'

Lisa saw the bitter look on Iliana's face. The further she stayed away from this triangle of intrigue the better. 'And who's the new zoologist?' she asked.

'I do not know. But if she is like Ginny she will not last one day. Guy needs someone who knows about elephants. The project has been very badly set back and time is short.'

'And what do you do?' Lisa asked.

'I'm the sound recordist, but what I really want to do is write the music.' She lifted her dark eyebrows. 'I also worked with Guy in South America. You may have seen *Extinction* — '

'Yes, I did! It won the top award last year. It was brilliant!'

'Thanks.' Iliana smiled, half closing her eyes. 'We worked well together, Guy and me. So when I heard he'd be doing this film I offered my services. What a man! I would do anything just to be with him.' She looked upwards, as though he would appear out of the clear blue sky.

Suddenly she narrowed her eyes. 'And you? Are you . . . what do you say? Attached? Engaged or anything?'

Lisa laughed. 'Good heavens, no. It's the last thing on my mind.'

Iliana breathed out, letting her arms fall to her sides as her face relaxed into a smile. 'Well, you have to meet the right man, I suppose.'

'Yes, I suppose you do,' Lisa said quietly.

But why was she listening to all this when she hadn't the slightest interest in the world's most famous wildlife filmmaker? She didn't even want to see him, though she realised this would be impossible to avoid. Still, with the adoring sound recordist drooling over him he wouldn't be much bothered about her. He'd proved once before that he wasn't, so why would he change after five years?

Iliana looked at her watch. 'Lisa, I must go. I have some recording to do. We are doing most of the sound wild. You know, separate, not linked to the

15

camera. Guy will be angry if I do not finish before he gets back. Come over before sunset tomorrow,' she said, then gave Lisa directions to Hippo Camp. 'Cover up well. And wear your boots. The mosquitoes will be biting. And you never know — sometimes the snakes too. But if you are worried about driving back in the dark, Tony could fetch you — '

'I'll be fine,' Lisa said, walking with Iliana to her vehicle. 'I know this area well.'

'Okay. See you tomorrow. I must hurry. Guy likes things done on schedule. I must not let him down.'

'Yes, of course,' she murmured.

Lisa watched Iliana's cloud of dust gradually disappear. So, nothing had changed. He still thinks everybody else can work as hard as he can. When he'd organised exhibitions for the Oxford University Photographic Society, he'd expected miracles from everyone. He always got what he wanted too, though goodness knows what it was about the man that commanded such devotion.

She had no answer to that, yet wasn't it partly this authority that had attracted her to him? It was a quality that had been missing in her life. No mother and a father who had totally ignored her, giving her no guidance or discipline — nothing, except money. Whereas Guy had made her feel that everything she did mattered to him.

No one had ever given her that feeling of security before. A Jekyll and Hyde if ever there was one, she'd discovered to her cost.

★　　★　　★

Lisa sat down on her stool and closed her eyes as she tried to sort out her tangled emotions. Confusion, longing, fear, but mostly anger. Anger for what he'd done to her, and anger that he should appear once more in her life. Yet she could not contain her curiosity at the prospect of seeing him again.

Over the years she'd watched his

films on TV, trying not to identify them with the man who had created them. She'd marvelled at the magical quality of his camera work, the seamless continuity of his scenes, the sensitive linking of close-up and distance shots, and the choice of music with just the right note of drama and pathos. But above all at the sense of passion and caring that shone through all his work.

Only someone special could make films like these. Can he have changed that much?

But she had work to do. Forcing Guy from her mind she packed her rucksack and fired up the Land Rover. She didn't want to lose track of the two pregnant elephants she'd been following, and precious minutes had already been lost. Monitoring their progress — and hopefully the births of their calves — would be vital for her present study.

But no matter how hard she tried, she could not get Guy out of her mind. The more she thought about him the more furious she became. She'd never be able to behave in a normal manner towards the man who had caused her such heartache. Who had humiliated her, led her on and then made her feel as worthless as her father had always done.

When she'd fled back to her college room all those years ago and picked up her suitcase, leaving no forwarding address for the long summer vacation, she'd been determined never to see him again. That was the end. She remembered the leering grin this morning from the helicopter window. If Guy Barrington had any other ideas, he could think again. Clearly he hadn't changed. A man already involved with Ginny somebody or other, and now Iliana . . .

Tomorrow, when she finally came face to face with him, how would she feel? Would she still hate him? Would she ever be able forget the hurt, the despair, the humiliation of that night, so engraved in her mind that she could see it now, right in front of her as though it were happening all over again . . .

2

It is Guy's final day at Oxford. The day she has been longing for because she knows it will be the happiest day of her life. It is the day he will tell her what she has waited for months to hear, and tomorrow they will be flying together to Brazil.

Her suitcase is packed with the new clothes bought with only one thing in mind — to please Guy. He still hasn't actually asked her to join him in Brazil, but knowing Guy — always full of last minute surprises himself — he will be thrilled to hear she has booked a seat for herself on the same flight as his.

Winning the National Geographic competition will take him out of England for a whole year, and maybe more, and after that wonderful night two weeks ago, she knows he will not want to leave her on her own.

She takes a shower, using the scented soap he gave her for her eighteenth birthday, its aroma as intoxicating as a bunch of newly picked roses. She brushes her hair until it is smooth and shiny, just the way he likes it. It is almost down to her waist now, but he won't hear of her cutting it. She wears the slinky black skirt he persuaded her to buy, and the red top he always insists on for the photographs he is forever taking of her.

It is a warm summer's night in late June, still broad daylight. She takes the short cut along the banks of the River Isis. It reminds her of the magical day he first took her punting, when he taught her how to photograph sunlight and shade . . .

Outside his flat she stops dead. The front door is open. Loud music is playing. Not the kind of music Guy likes. Crowds of people are talking and laughing.

But this was supposed to be just the two of them. 'Come round on Friday night,' he had said, 'and wear something special. We'll have a drink, maybe go out to eat . . . ' and his voice had trailed off, leaving her to imagine the rest.

She walks in. The photograph of her in the red top is no longer on the passage wall. Well, of course, he must have packed it, ready for their new life in Brazil. In the next room she glimpses Monica, her thick blonde plait flying around as she dances. She hasn't told her she won't be coming back next term. In fact she's told no one yet. She wanted it to be a surprise . . .

In the kitchen people are putting little pieces of cheese on sticks and taking steaming sausage rolls out of the oven. Guy has a lot of friends, but what are they all doing here?

Suddenly she hears Guy's voice coming from upstairs. She is just about to run up the stairs to see him when she hears a woman's voice too. A voice she doesn't recognise.

Slowly she walks up the stairs, her

heart beating wildly.

'I'm so sorry,' she hears Guy say. 'You should have phoned me. I'd have come at once.' Then silence.

She takes a few steps towards the bedroom, before she sees them.

His back is towards her, hair awry, shirt off one shoulder.

Inside the circle of his arms is Sally Lomas from the PS. Not one of their regular crowd but a good photographer who has won many prizes. Her face buried in his neck, eyes tightly closed, red hair draped all over him.

For a few moments she watches them, unable to move, unable to speak. The she turns and hurtles down the stairs as though she is leaping off a cliff.

Out on the road she keeps running. Back in her room she bangs down the lid of her suitcase, squashing the now useless pile of new clothes. She rings for a taxi, her fingers shaking, her head spinning with disbelief.

The taxi driver smiles. 'Where to, love?'

'The station,' she says, as they drive along the familiar Oxford streets. Streets she never wants to see again because every one reminds her of Guy.

'Going somewhere exciting?' the driver asks.

'Er . . . yes.' She doesn't know yet, and doesn't care. All she knows is that she must get away from here, as far away as possible.

At the ticket desk the BR man waits patiently. She can't go home. Her father wouldn't understand. Where can she go?

She remembers her father's neglected cottage in the wilds of the Brecon Beacons. She still has the key. Yes, I will go there. I will climb the soaring heights of the Pen-y-Fan and vanish off the face of the earth forever . . .

* * *

The two pregnant elephant cows, escorted by their entourage of protective aunts and sisters, crossed the wide muddy river early that afternoon. The river formed the eastern boundary of the game reservation area, but elephants knew no limits and this made Enoch and Lisa's job more than usually hazardous.

First they had to drive north to the village of Sumba, a small group of thatched huts near the water's edge. Crossing on the pontoon, they entered the remote Chilangola Woodlands, where last year Lisa did most of her research with the World Wildlife team. She knew every path and shady glade — and almost every elephant.

She was glad they had made the effort, though on the way back the pontoon seemed more rickety than usual.

'Look out, Lisa!' Enoch said, scuttling to the centre of the raft as the water lapped the edges of the flimsy structure.

Lisa tried not to think of the new Land Rover and all the precious equipment being swept down the river. She even pretended not to see the horny grey humps of the crocodiles

25

sunning themselves on the sandy banks, their half-closed eyes watching her every move, or the beady eyes and twitching ears of the snorting hippos as they cruised along the riverbed.

The following day they went back to the Chilangola Woodlands, leaving before sunrise and returning in mid-afternoon to give Lisa a chance to freshen up before her visit to Hippo Camp. The pontoon seemed even more fragile. Enoch had pulled a wry face and Lisa wondered if she would have to abandon the cows if they insisted on staying on that side of the river.

After washing off the day's dust Lisa brushed her hair in the sun until it shone like polished ebony. She tucked her slim fitting cotton trousers into her mosquito boots and set off in her Land Rover, more nervous than she'd been for years.

Perched on the banks of the river, Hippo Camp had a well-established, settled feel to it. Iliana led her to a table with green canvas chairs arranged beneath the wide-spreading branches of an enormous wild fig tree. There was no sign of Guy.

'They're not long back,' Iliana said, seeing Lisa's puzzled expression. 'They've just gone to shower.' She cocked her head to one side. 'You didn't tell me you knew Guy.'

'It was a long time ago,' Lisa said. 'It didn't seem important. I didn't think he'd remember me.'

'*Remember* you?' Iliana raised one eyebrow, then lowered her head and peered at Lisa through half closed eyes. 'He remembered you all right. He saw you from the helicopter. He knew immediately it was you. What did you *do* to him?'

Lisa turned towards the river. Iliana's tone was not as friendly as it had been yesterday morning, she thought, twisting her fingers behind her back as she gazed at the shimmering water.

'Why, what did he say?' she asked, still pretending to look at the sunset but acutely aware of Iliana's dark eyes glaring at her.

'He hasn't stopped talking about you since he arrived back from Lusaka. Anyway, you can find out for yourself. Here he comes now.'

Lisa swallowed hard, took a deep breath, then turned and watched him walk towards her.

He was leaner than she remembered. The sun had bleached his hair and bronzed his skin since his last TV appearance, and he seemed even taller than when he'd been at Oxford. A new vertical line was etched on either side of his mouth.

'Hello Lisa.'

For a few moments he stared at her, his lips pursed, his eyes steady. Then he laughed and shook his head as though he still couldn't believe it was her.

'What a surprise! I could hardly believe our luck when I saw you yesterday morning.'

Luck? Lisa wondered what luck had to do with it. She'd been an idiot to accept the invitation. She could have made up any excuse rather than put herself through this ordeal.

'Yes,' she said. 'It's a surprise to see you too.'

'You're even more beautiful, if I may say so.' He held Lisa's hand with more than the accepted pressure for a social greeting. 'And you've cut your hair — '

'It's more practical for the bush — '

'Guy!' Iliana's voice had a note of irritation Lisa had not heard before. 'There are drinks to be poured and I'm sure Lisa wants to hear all about the film.'

Guy slid his fingers to Lisa's elbow and guided her to a chair. Without taking his eyes off her he walked to the other side of the table where a small gas fridge stood on a wooden base beside the massive fig-tree trunk. He poured ice-cold mango juices for Lisa and Iliana and sat down with a can of lager for himself.

'Am I glad you're here!' he said, giving all his attention to Lisa as though

Iliana no longer existed.

He could get away with murder when he looked at you like that, Lisa thought warily. After tonight she would avoid this camp. She had work to do and she had no intention of letting Guy Barrington interfere with it.

'What did you do with the mail bag, Guy?'

Lisa turned to see the smiling sunburned face of a man somewhere in his early thirties. He had a towel in his hand and was drying his long dark hair.

'Oh, I'm sorry,' he said, smoothing his tousled head as he spotted Lisa. 'I didn't realise we had company already.'

'This is Tony Greer,' Guy said. 'When he gets that mop of his combed, he can come and be sociable.'

Lisa liked the look of Tony, a tall, lanky man with smiling eyes and a long mobile face. He was clearly under Guy's thumb, but that's exactly how it had been at Oxford. Everybody running around Guy as though he were some kind of god. Well, she would never get caught in that trap again. She had her own life to lead, and it didn't include Guy Barrington.

'Tony's not only a fantastic journalist *and* a pilot,' Guy said when Tony reappeared with his hair neatly combed. 'He's a wizard at barbecues. Between them he and Iliana provide the best gourmet food in Africa.'

Lisa looked around the tented camp. 'Don't you have a cook? There seem to be plenty of helpers around.'

'Joseph and all the other staff are excellent. But I like the personal touch now and then.' He winked at Iliana.

Yes, I'm sure you do, Lisa thought, noticing Iliana's adoring gaze. 'But don't Tony and Iliana have more important duties?'

'Got to keep them busy,' he said, with another sideways glance at Iliana. 'Otherwise they'd get up to no good.'

In the ensuing pause Lisa sensed the underlying tension between these talented filmmakers.

'And what about you?' she asked

Guy, relieved that their conversation was on such a banal level.

'Me?' He leaned back and sipped his beer. 'You should know, Lisa. I keep the show on the road. And believe me, it's a full time job.'

He drew the fingers of his left hand slowly across his lips, then took a deep breath and held it while he turned and looked at Lisa.

'But you know, Lisa, this is fate working in a most mysterious way. Wouldn't you agree?'

'What d'you mean?'

'You! Showing up here like this.' He put one elbow on the table and cupped his chin in his hand. 'It's almost as though you had known.'

'Known what?' she said, highly suspicious of his tone of *fait accompli*.

'That Ginny would desert me for the comforts of civilisation, and the academic my London office recruited would change her mind at the last minute to do research in Botswana. I waited two hours at the airport this morning, then found her letter in my mail bag telling me she wasn't coming!'

'Guy, I haven't the faintest idea what you're talking about.'

'Ginny's replacement. She'd have been no good anyway. Ginny wasn't right either, even if she'd been able to take the mosquitoes and the tsetse flies and the rough living. The camp in Brazil was luxurious compared to this.' He grasped Lisa's hand.

'If only I'd known you were available all along!' He lifted his eyebrows and twisted round to face her. 'I've followed your career, you know. It's just too incredible. You see, Lisa my dear, you're the one for this job — '

Lisa jerked her hand away, then steeled herself to meet Guy's gaze. If she didn't put her foot down straight away she'd be lost.

'I'm sorry to disappoint you, Guy. But I'm afraid that I am *not* available.'

3

'Lisa,' Guy said quietly, a self-satisfied smile on his lips. 'You're here, aren't you?'

'Yes,' she said, with a smile to equal his. 'But I have my own project and I can't possibly abandon it.'

'I never thought I'd have to spell it out to you, of all people. I thought you were dedicated to saving the elephant. I *know* you are,' he added, with a distant look in his eyes that told Lisa there wasn't much he had forgotten.

Guy says jump and everyone jumps. She remembered how his devoted disciples, including herself, had fallen under his spell. But all that was over a long time ago.

'I'm sorry, Guy. I'm here to do a specific study. I can't possibly drop it. KEA Group is funding me — '

'With your own money — '

Guy drew in his breath and slapped his hand to his mouth. 'Forgive me, Lisa.' He closed his eyes, then slowly opened them again, his brow creased in a look of genuine regret. 'I was truly sorry to hear about your father's death. But unfortunately the media reports were very candid. Everyone knows he left everything to you.'

When Lisa said nothing he tilted his head to one side. 'If you write out another cheque for KEA,' he said, looking slightly uncomfortable, 'I'm sure they'll be perfectly happy to release you for a few weeks.'

Lisa shook her head.

'Besides,' he said, trailing his finger-tips slowly up her arm. 'Think what fun it'll be to work together. Like old times, huh?'

'Never!' Lisa said, snatching her arm away. The memory of her father's obsession with making money and buying people's love and respect, including hers, was still too painful to discuss. Guy was probably right, but she was furious that he should assume the money she had inherited was available on tap.

'Lisa . . . ?'

She knew that tone. Low, soft, pleading, with a little catch at the back of the throat. She turned away. It would be easier if she didn't have to see his eyes.

Blast him. He'd overstepped the mark and now he was trying to make amends, though that didn't stop the effect his voice was having on her. His voice, and the feel of his fingertips on her skin . . .

For a few moments she closed her eyes, letting the final orange glow of the sun caress her eyelids while memories of those sonorous tones seeped unbidden into her consciousness.

Behind her, no one spoke as they all waited for her answer. She heard Iliana and Tony move discreetly away — no doubt in answer to Guy's silent command.

She turned to look at him again. The

muscles around his eyes had tensed, reducing them to narrow slits that focused on her, silently pleading for an answer. She felt as though she was caught in the beam of a hunter's lamp on a moonless night, with nowhere to run.

'Anyway,' she said, determined not to succumb. 'What makes you think it'll be fun to work with you?'

Slowly, with as much tenderness as if he were rescuing a baby bird that had fallen out of its nest, he took her hand in his.

Lisa recognised long-forgotten sensations stirring in her body. Not in five long years had she known even the slightest twinge of what she felt now. And it frightened her.

'There was a time, wasn't there, Lisa, when you'd have dropped everything to be with me.'

Even his voice had slowed down. Just like it always had when he'd allowed his emotions to over-rule his normal reserve. She could still see, as though it was yesterday, the way he would slowly lift his head until their eyes met, just as he was doing now. He would edge towards her, so gradually that when finally he touched her it was like a pain shooting from the tips of her fingers to the ends of her toes.

Then in complete contrast to this mellifluous conquest of her senses, he would abruptly move away, frowning and sighing deeply and shaking his head.

For months she had lived on this knife-edge of anticipation, until at last, on that one and only occasion, her dreams had almost come true.

Guy lifted his eyebrows as though inviting an acknowledgement of his outrageous statement. Dropped everything? In order to be with him? But how could he possibly have known how close she'd been to doing just that? When she'd seen him with Sally Lomas she'd turned and fled and they hadn't seen each other again — until now? How could he have known?

'You're quite wrong,' she said.

'Really, Lisa?'

'Yes. *Really*. And it's just as well I didn't — '

'What do you mean?'

Lisa felt as if she'd been shoved against a wall with a firing squad lined up in front of her. She had vowed never to let this conversation take place, and here she was, in danger of baring wounds that even now had not healed.

'Nothing,' she said.

Guy sat absolutely still, half closing his eyes as though remembering something he would rather forget.

'Why did you walk out on me?' he asked with a sudden tremor in his voice that Lisa had heard only once before — the night they had held in their hands the little ivory carving of an elephant, when they had discovered their mutual anguish for animals under threat.

He moved closer. His knees were almost touching hers.

'An explanation would have been the

polite thing to do, instead of disappearing without any trace.' He reached for her hands. 'You knew I was flying to South America the next day.'

The eerie silence was like the moments before an African storm. You knew something was going to happen but not when it would happen or how fierce it would be.

'Well?' he said.

She wrenched her hands free. 'If you don't mind, I'd rather not talk about that night.'

He took one step towards her. She felt trapped. She looked around the darkening shadows of the camp. The smoke drifting from the fires carried a tantalising aroma of meat barbecued over charcoal, and she wished Tony and Iliana would hurry up and return with the food.

'If you must know, Guy, I did the only thing left for me to do. I'm sure it made things a lot simpler for us both — '

'Don't let him bully you, Lisa,' Iliana

said, hurrying towards them with a tray of colourful salads arranged like a surrealistic work of art. 'When he gets that serious look on his face it's time to watch out.'

She stopped next to Guy and nudged against him. 'Tony's giving the steaks their final turn. Perhaps you could replenish the drinks.'

Lisa sensed Iliana's resentment at leaving her and Guy alone while she and Tony prepared the meal. 'Is there anything I can do?' she volunteered, wishing she had asked earlier.

'Not tonight,' Guy said. 'Tonight you're a guest. When you move into camp you can go on the roster. So make the most of it,' he said with a half smile on his face that Lisa knew meant he was deadly serious.

Iliana banged the tray onto the table. Still holding the handles she spun her head round to look at Guy.

Lisa felt sorry for Iliana. Guy had clearly not changed. He was still exactly like her father had been, with a different girlfriend every few weeks. What a set-up, she thought, thankful that she was not any part of it.

'Well?' Guy said. 'When are you moving over, Lisa?'

'Never,' she said.

Yet in one way she was tempted. When Monica King had offered her this assignment she had welcomed the idea of having no one to influence her particular style of research. After only three days she'd realised the folly of electing to work alone.

She took a few steps towards the swirling river. Hippos grunted like oboes tuning up as they lumbered up the grassy banks where they would spend the night. In the distance a lion roared. In spite of the vastness of this wide open paradise, Lisa felt trapped in the web of this man whose power had always encompassed everyone in his orbit.

'Man was not born to be a loner,' Guy said softly.

She swung round. His eyes were

crinkling up at the corners in the way she had once thought was a smile he gave to no one else but her. How unnerving that he could still read her thoughts.

'For heaven's sake, Lisa, even the elephants stick together, give each other support. You can't go on living on your own. Besides, it's dangerous.'

Dangerous? Nothing was more dangerous than being in a situation where she could become an involuntary pawn in a tug-of-war over this man.

Be firm, she told herself, but act as nonchalantly as possible.

'Rubbish! I have the best game ranger in the country. And I wouldn't dream of imposing on your hospitality.'

'You wouldn't be imposing, Lisa. And just because you went to boarding school at the age of eight, and learned not to depend on other people, doesn't mean you have to carry that early responsibility for your own well-being into the rest of your life.'

Lisa blinked. Although not strictly

true, she was taken aback by the depth of his perception. How much else of their casual conversations had he remembered?

'It's kind of you to feel sorry for me,' she said, keeping her eyes averted but unable to stop herself looking back at him. 'But I'd never get any work done if I moved in here. I have my own agenda.'

He stared at her, clearly waiting for her capitulation.

'Besides, I'd only be a nuisance,' she said with an exaggerated smile. 'You see, I'm quite useless at domestic chores. Especially cooking.'

'Absolute nonsense!' Guy said. 'We need a zoologist and we need one now. The rains start in November. We're half way through October. You can feel the heat building up. We're working against the clock. Heavy rain and mud would halt our shoot — '

Lisa put up her hands in protest but Guy carried on.

'We need your help, Lisa. We'd all

hoped the poaching was dying down. Then a few days ago, what did I see?' He banged his fists on the sides of his head. 'Another tuskless carcass. With a week old baby next to it. Starving from lack of milk in spite of a whole family of would-be foster mothers urging the poor little thing to keep standing — '

Lisa was hardly breathing. She was thinking about the unborn calves whose mothers she had followed for two days, perhaps doomed never to survive their first year. Or even their first week.

'Are we going to sit back, Lisa, and watch that happening? And do nothing about it?'

She closed her eyes, remembering the little ivory elephant they had held together . . .

'Lisa?'

She looked up at Guy and saw the same compassion in his eyes that five years ago had changed her life.

'Without you,' he whispered, 'this film — and all it will mean for the preservation of the elephant — will be doomed.'

Lisa swallowed hard. 'Such flattery will get you nowhere,' she said, attempting against her innate sensibilities to keep her refusal light-hearted. 'But seriously, I have a tight schedule. I must also finish before the rains. I can't help you but I'm sure you'll get someone else soon.'

'Guy, what about Jean-Paul?' Iliana said, waltzing around the table with the knives and forks, clearly elated by Lisa's negative decision. 'He can spare a few weeks before he goes back to Brazil — and he likes elephants — '

'I don't *want* Jean-Paul,' Guy said. 'It must be someone who *loves* elephants. Who can help me to understand their behaviour. Interpret what they're doing. Identify the individuals and tell me where they're going and *why* — '

Throughout this tirade his eyes had remained fixed on Lisa's. 'How can you, of all people, let down a project that could prevent further needless loss of elephants?'

Lisa held her breath, moved by the passion in every word he uttered.

'I don't believe it. You are not the Lisa Ryding I knew at Oxford. What happened to her?'

'That's a good question,' she whispered.

She knew he was right, but how could she tell him that five years ago the old Lisa Ryding had died and that like the proverbial phoenix a new one had risen from her ashes. A new Lisa Ryding who was immune to the velvet voice, the special smile, the sapphire eyes, the sensuous mouth . . .

At that moment Tony appeared with a tray of sizzling steaks and sausages. 'Help yourselves, you lot,' he said, putting his arm around Iliana and giving her a friendly little kiss on her cheek. 'The cooks need a cold beer after that.'

The meal was devoured in almost complete silence, intensifying the magical sounds of the night. No more was said about Lisa abandoning her job to help with the film, although she felt the threat hanging over her.

When they had finished she helped to clear the table. 'Thank you. That was a terrific meal.' She turned to Tony, who was sitting gazing at Iliana. 'And what fantastic sausages!'

'*Boerewors*,' Tony said. 'Lean beef. Fatty pork. Coriander. No breadcrumbs or water to ruin the texture. Cooked on high heat to preserve the juices . . . '

'You could have it every day,' Guy said. 'It's part of our regular diet.'

But Lisa did not respond to the bait.

'I hope you don't mind if I leave now,' she said quickly. 'It takes me a week or two to acclimatise to the altitude, and I just can't get enough sleep.'

Guy leapt up and stood at her side. 'I'll see you home,' he said, just as naturally as he had done in Oxford after their weekly meetings of the Photographic Society. 'I'll follow you in the Cruiser.'

'Thanks, but I'll be fine. It's not far.'

'Don't wait for me,' he told the others. 'Lisa and I have a lot to talk about. Come on,' he said, 'I'll lead the way. See you stay right behind me.'

Guy had never lacked chivalry. He was attentive almost to the point of being labelled old fashioned. He had always made her feel special when he took her out. Sometimes in Oxford he had arrived at their appointed meeting place with a bunch of flowers, often a single rose — nothing elaborate, but done with such charm that she would feel as though nothing in the whole world could make her happier. On Oxford's busy streets he would walk on the outside of the pavement, his fingers touching hers. In a pub or a restaurant he would always stand until she was seated.

But chivalry was not everything, she recalled ruefully.

Suddenly through the maze of trees and grass she saw his brake lights flashing.

She stopped. A moment later he jumped out of the Cruiser and climbed in beside her, closing the door quietly and sliding his arm along the back of her seat.

'You were very quiet tonight, Lisa. Are you feeling okay?'

Oh, that voice, the tenderness, just the way he'd spoken to her all those years ago . . .

'I'm fine,' she said, keeping her eyes directly in front of her. She felt the cool decisive touch of his fingers as they drifted down to her arm. It had often puzzled her why he had always seemed to go out of his way to make sure that she was safe, even when it wasn't necessary, making contact, making sure she wouldn't be hurt.

How naive she'd been! Straight out of boarding school. No mother to warn her of the ways of men. Only her own yearning for love, and in her dreams a fantasy man who encompassed all the dreamiest pop stars whose pictures she'd tacked to her bed-sit walls at boarding school. She'd never had a boyfriend. Didn't want one if they were going to treat you the way her father had treated her mother. But that hadn't stopped her growing need to love someone, and have someone love her. Even then she knew there was no such person, but as long as she only dreamed, she would be safe . . .

Until one day, soon after she'd arrived at Oxford, at the first meeting of the Photographic Society that her friend Monica had taken her to, there he was.

Her fantasy man in the flesh.

Even now she could picture the exact moment she had first seen him.

'Monica,' she'd said, struggling to gain her breath. 'Who is *that?*'

Monica had followed her gaze. Being three years older she was often critical of Lisa's naivety and lack of normal streetwise attributes.

'The one in the cream sweater,' Lisa prompted, pointing to the living image of the fantasy man she'd conjured up at school.

'Oh! You mean Guy Barrington?' Monica had said.

'But who is he?' she insisted.

'I wouldn't bother, Lisa. He'll break your heart. He's at least fifteen years older than you are. Ex City lawyer. Final year engineering. Best photographer in this society. Wins all the prizes. Nobody knows much about him. Never seems to get close to anyone. Not for long, anyway. Rumour is he was once married. Had one child that died. But he won't talk about this. Not to anyone. Disappears for weekends now and then. A bit of a mystery, really. But out of your league, kid.'

'Yes, but . . . ' she had insisted.

'Lisa, take my advice. He is not to be had for love or money.'

'But he's been looking at me ever since we came in. Just staring.'

'He looks at every pretty girl, but it never lasts,' Monica had whispered. 'Stop staring at him. You're only encouraging him and it'll get you nowhere. Come on, let's see if we can sort out this fantastic new camera of yours. What a beaut it is!'

Monica was fiddling with the Leica when suddenly there was someone standing in front of them.

'Correct me if I'm wrong,' he said. 'But is that the latest single lens reflex?'

Lisa had nodded, hating her shyness. Monica shrugged her shoulders, handed Lisa the camera and walked away.

'Do you mind if I have a look?' He held the camera as though it was a priceless ornament about to be auctioned at Sotheby's, turning it round and looking at it from every angle.

'I'm afraid I have no idea how to use it,' Lisa said boldly.

He whistled softly. 'Where did you get it?'

'My father gave it to me for passing my entrance exams.'

He looked up from the camera and smiled, nodding his approval.

'Are you an expert on Leicas?' she asked.

'You could call me an enthusiast, I

suppose. Why do you ask?'

'I just wondered. I mean, if you aren't too busy — '

'I would be delighted to help a beautiful girl learn how to use her oh so beautiful camera. But I'm afraid I don't know your name.'

'Lisa Ryding,' she'd said.

'Any relation to *the* Richard Ryding?'

She had always hated admitting her relationship to her notorious father, almost more famous for his romantic escapades than for his acquisition of one of the country's major newspapers. She nodded.

He held out his hand. 'Guy Barrington,' he announced with a slight tilt of his head and a clicking of his heels.

His grip was firm but gentle, his fingers long and strong. As they lingered in the palm of her hand, Lisa felt something strange happening to her, like no other feeling she'd ever had before.

'I'm running a special studio session next Friday. Two till six at The

Photographer's Workshop. I'll put you down for a place and we can start to unravel the mysteries of your Leica.' He handed her the camera. 'Well,' he said, touching her arm, leaving it there until she could feel the heat of his fingers. 'I'll see you on Friday.' He turned and walked away. Just before he reached the door he twisted his head around and looked at her again . . .

He was touching her arm now, here, in the middle of the African bush, and Lisa realised with a shock that nothing had changed. Without conscious effort she had slipped back five years, eclipsing time and distance, anger and hurt. She could feel the energy in his fingers that came right from the centre of him, doing to her the same crazy things it had always done.

She could smell the wood smoke on his face, mingled with an aromatic after-shave. Even here in the bush he was perfectly groomed, just as he'd been in those heady Oxford days when he hadn't been able to walk into a room or down a street without drawing every female head towards him.

Suddenly, through the open window of the Land Rover, she heard a rhythmic crackling of dry grass and twigs. Guy gripped her arm.

'Shh! Don't move. Keep dead still.'

'What? I can't see anything . . . '

'Look through that gap. There, towards the river!'

As she turned, she felt his breath on her cheek. It was like the touch of a petal in a field of wild flowers. 'Yes,' she murmured, amazed that her sharp eyes had not seen the elephants before he had. 'I see them now. There must be at least nine or ten, and probably a few calves.'

'How can you even contemplate letting them down, Lisa?'

'Please, let's talk about this some other time. I'd like to get back to my camp.'

Lisa was alarmed at how close the elephants were since they had first spotted them. But she was far more alarmed at what Guy's closeness was doing to her. She pulled away. 'Let's move on,' she whispered. 'Elephants have become nervous of human beings, especially at night. The scent of a poacher as much as two miles away can send a herd stampeding down on them — '

'Don't be silly,' he whispered. 'We're not poachers.'

'No, but if they're frightened or provoked they will defend themselves.'

'Lisa, this is the family I've been filming for several weeks now. They've grown accustomed to my vehicle. Besides, we're upwind of them — '

'Yes, but they have fantastic hearing, so let's go.'

★   ★   ★

Arriving a few minutes later at Lisa's camp, Guy looked around at the meagre amenities. 'I'm not having you staying here, Lisa. Tomorrow I'll help you move to Hippo Camp.'

'Thanks for a lovely evening,' she said, edging away from him. 'I live mostly on tinned food and pawpaw, so that was a treat. Please don't waste any more time. I'm sure you have things to do — '

He took a step towards her. 'I'm not going until you come to your senses.'

'If you think I'm going to abandon my project just to take the place of ... of your ... of the zoologist who decided to leave you in the lurch, then — '

'Ah, so that's it!'

Guy took hold of Lisa's shoulders as once more she tried to slip away. 'Lisa, you're not jealous, are you?' There was an anxious tone to his voice and a look of concern in his eyes.

'Jealous! I have everything I want and even if I didn't I wouldn't be looking for it anywhere near you!' She bit her lip, wishing she could take back her words. Yet wasn't it partly jealousy that had made her run from his flat? Jealousy that he had abandoned her for someone else?

Yes, but things were different now, she told herself. Jealousy was a childish trait resulting from her early insecurity. It had no place in her adult world of scientific study. A world that for her was complete, without the interference of complicated relationships.

Suddenly Guy let go of her. 'You know, Lisa, I thought I knew you.'

The music of the African night was all around them but Lisa could hear nothing but the throb of her heart and the rasp of Guy's breath as he stood next to her, his arms hanging limply at his sides.

'What happened to you, Lisa? What are you afraid of? Why are you hiding here all alone?' He gestured to her solitary tent.

Lisa shook her head, trembling as she thought of the impact Guy had had on her life. When she'd gone up to Oxford, not knowing who she was or where she was going, he had given her a pathway. He had helped to mould her future career, and for the first time she had known the tender care of another human being . . .

'Say yes, Lisa. Without your help I'll never get this film completed. And I think you know what that means. It is scheduled for worldwide release. It'll be shown to millions, in all the countries where ivory is still sold and used. And in those African countries where the thoughtless abuse of the habitat could still have catastrophic results for the elephants. Your knowledge and compassion could make all the difference. Don't let them down.'

Lisa fought to control the conflict within her. She knew the film was vital, and that her own project would not suffer from being delayed a few weeks. But how often had she promised herself that she would never again allow herself to be manipulated.

Guy was standing absolutely still. He had always known when to be silent.

If she said yes, there would have to be rules. Her rules. She would not become involved with him in any way but a strictly professional one. It would be on her terms, and hers alone.

'Give me a day or two to think about it, Guy. I'll have to ask the KEA Group to let me postpone my project. I'm sure they won't agree but I'll phone them tomorrow and let you know. But if I do — it'll only be for the elephants.'

'But my dear girl, what other reason could there be?'

4

It was approaching dawn when Lisa finally gave up any hope of sleep. A faint orange glow in the east had already dimmed the stars, but Jupiter was shining brightly like a miniature moon. The smell of wood smoke from Enoch's fire drifted into her tent, and the egrets and herons were beginning to stir.

Quickly she washed and dressed. The sooner she contacted Keep Elephants Alive, the better. With her mobile phone well out of range she would have to drive to the remote Kilanga rest camp fifteen miles downstream, where she hoped the one and only land telephone in the area would be working.

The grizzled old man who ran the rest camp was delighted to see Lisa and poured her a welcoming cup of coffee. After dialling only once, she was through to Monica King, who was now the organising secretary of KEA in London and had remained Lisa's closest friend.

Quickly she explained her predicament, certain that Monica would insist on her continuing her work.

'Lisa, I can't tell you what to do, but surely it's a great opportunity — '

'That's not the point, Monica. My work for KEA comes first — '

'Lisa, I don't know why you're even asking me. Those prize-winning films of Guy's have terrific impact. Lisa? Can you hear me? This line is terrible. The Barrington film will be an important boost just at the right time. Our project can wait.' She paused. 'Have you seen him yet?' she asked, her sudden change of tone echoing the concern she had always had for Lisa.

'Yes. I have.'

'And?'

'That's all in the past, Monica. He is nothing to me now. You know that.'

'Hmm. Well . . . be careful. I know

how tough you've become but I also know Guy Barrington. And if . . . '

'Don't worry, Monica. I can take care of myself. And thanks. I'll see you in London in December.'

'Good luck. I wish I were the one out in the field where all the action is. Instead of stuck here in London in an over-heated office . . . '

The line finally went dead. Driving back to camp, Lisa's mind churned with indecision. She felt as if someone had wound a rubber tube around her chest and was pumping it up.

The way is clear, but do you really want to commit yourself to three weeks of close contact with Guy Barrington?

Yes, of course I do, a voice said inside her head.

But is that sensible?

No, of course it isn't.

And do you think Guy will take no for an answer?

It will be futile to refuse. Besides, you must be honest. You want to help with the film, don't you?

Do I?

Of course you do. And if Guy is going to have the slightest chance of meeting that deadline for the TV premiere, how can you refuse?

Oh for heaven's sake . . .

Arriving at her campsite, she was no nearer a decision. Anyway, there was a crucial observation she needed to make this morning and it wouldn't do Guy any harm to wait another day for her answer.

The temperature was already in the high eighties. She parked under the ebony tree, then quickly changed into khaki shorts and the boots she always wore on her field trips. She collected her equipment, made sure her water bottle was filled, persuaded Enoch to take the morning off to spend with his family, then headed south.

Approaching the area where yesterday she thought she had glimpsed newly born twins, she slowed down. Apart from the steady screech of cicadas, the only other sound was the crunch of tyres on the dry cracked ground. She stopped in the shade of a grove of acacia trees the elephants had not yet mutilated, then quietly opened the door of the Land Rover, crouched down, and waited.

There was no guarantee they would pass along this trail today, but without warning, there they were.

Through the long yellow grass she saw the mother, recognisable by her unusually short body and the jagged slit in her right ear. And with her was a newly born calf.

It was a thrilling sight, but where was the other twin?

Sensing the imminent arrival of further female members of the family, Lisa climbed back into the Land Rover. She waited for several minutes, but still the second twin did not appear.

Disappointed, she started the engine, but quickly switched it off when another female, also with a newly born calf in tow, came into view. Lisa held her breath.

Yes! The babies were the same size and had the same pattern of tight curly black hair on their foreheads. She had never observed young twins at such close quarters before, and oh, how adorable they were!

This was just what Guy should be filming, she thought, and when they began to suckle she crept out of the Land Rover and started photographing them from every possible angle. If nothing else, Guy could use these stills in the film . . .

Suddenly there was a commotion behind her. Three older females were advancing, their trunks waving high in the air. Instinct told her not to run but their body language was telling her they were extremely angry.

'Lisa! This way!'

Guy?

What was he doing here?

Blindly she obeyed his voice, leaping headlong through the long grass, heedless of its sharp edges slashing her arms and face.

'This way, Lisa!' he shouted. '*Run!*'

Gasping for breath, she glanced over her shoulder. The elephants were almost upon her. Even though these massive beasts didn't run, they could easily out-walk a champion sprinter.

Seconds seemed like minutes. Stars swam before her eyes but she kept on running. Blindly she followed Guy's voice but instead of it becoming louder it grew fainter. Soon she couldn't even make out the direction or the words clearly . . .

Just as blackness was about to envelop her she felt a jolt to her body and the air was expelled from her lungs.

Guy had intercepted her flight and was half carrying, half dragging her along the ground. As they reached his Land Cruiser he hurled her onto the front seat and leapt in beside her.

A moment later they were hurtling headlong into the trackless bush, Guy's feet flashing up and down on the driving pedals as he manoeuvred the four-by-four like a bucking bronco over the uneven terrain.

Branches crashed into the fenders and lashed the windscreen as the vehicle ploughed through trees and bushes, swerving and lurching so that Lisa had to hold on tightly to Guy's legs to keep from falling through the empty space where the door usually was.

Finally they stopped. Dust poured in and swirled around them. Lisa remained where she was, smarting from the cuts on her face and limbs. The dust overtook them, then slowly settled.

Guy gently wiped the hair from her eyes. Sheepishly she turned and looked at him. His hair was matted with perspiration. His shirt was open and torn, revealing a gaping gash on his chest.

'I'm sorry,' she said. 'I didn't realise . . . '

'You silly idiot. You were almost killed.'

'So were you. You risked your life.'

'Rubbish,' he said. Then his tone

softened. 'Why the hell did you get out of the Land Rover? And why did you turn off the ignition?'

'It starts easily. It's brand new. I wanted to get the twins from every angle — '

'You could have, if you'd been patient enough. You can't be in a hurry when you photograph wildlife.'

'But I might have missed them altogether. I couldn't risk doing that.'

'Well, you've ruined *my* shots!'

Lisa bit down on her bottom lip. 'Oh no. Were you — filming the twins?'

'Too right I was. I doubt we can ever go back there now. But more than that, there was an imminent birth.'

He looked upwards in a gesture of resignation, but she knew that underneath this facade of complacency he was burning with anger and disappointment.

'I've made an awful mess of things,' she said. 'I don't know why. I've been on my own often and nothing like this has ever happened before.'

'Well, it's obvious you can't be left alone any longer,' he said, not unkindly, although he had every reason to be furious. 'It's also fairly obvious that we should be working together. At least then you wouldn't ruin shots I've had set up for hours. I doubt I'll ever get that close to another birth.'

'I'm so sorry, Guy. But I think I know where we might have another chance . . . '

'And twins must be pretty rare too,' he said.

'Okay. I broke the rules, I know. But elephants aren't usually aggressive unless their young are being threatened. At the time I didn't think I was doing that.' She looked at him sheepishly. 'But I'm sure they'll quite happily accept you again. It's *my* vehicle they're not ever going to tolerate.'

'Lisa, it's my guess your beautiful new Land Rover will be never be the same again.'

She closed her eyes. This really was a mess. How on earth was she going to carry on without her Land Rover? 'I hope you're wrong,' she said.

'I hope so, too. Anyway, you won't need it from now on. You're moving over to Hippo Camp today and I want you in the Land Cruiser with me every day — not swanning off on your own.'

Lisa was past arguing. She dusted herself off, trying to regain her dignity after having been more frightened than she'd ever been in her life. She hated having it spelled out to her in this didactic way of Guy's, but what alternative did she have?

They moved off slowly, in complete contrast to the hair-raising speed at which they had just bolted through the bush.

'By the way,' Guy said. 'Did you get through to KEA?'

Lisa hesitated, still reluctant to commit herself.

'Monica's running it now, isn't she?' he said.

She nodded. Common sense told her she had no choice. And apart from any other consideration, she now owed it to Guy to guide him to the two pregnant cows that had crossed to the other side of the river — to the territory she knew so well.

'They agreed I could delay my project for a few weeks,' she said, keeping her voice as impersonal as she could.

'Great! We'll put you on the pay roll from today.'

'No, please don't do that. My board and keep is enough.'

'Nonsense. Your name will be on the credits. You'll have to accept a salary.'

★　★　★

As they drew up at her camp Lisa was at a loss for words. What do you say to a person who has just saved your life? The sight of his torn clothing and dishevelled hair prompted her to glance at herself in the mirror on the sun visor. Dusty and bedraggled, her face was streaked with dust and criss-crossed with red weals from the slashing grass.

'What a sight we look!' she said, bursting into laughter that was verging on the hysterical.

'Well, I'm not surprised,' Guy said, smiling down at her. Then suddenly his lips parted. He drew in his breath sharply. 'You always were, you know.'

'What?'

'A sight for sore eyes.'

Lisa sensed a quickening of her heartbeat. She had heard those exact words before.

'But somehow, out here in the open, with your hair all ruffled and your skin glowing, you look even lovelier than I remember. When I saw you from the helicopter I very nearly asked Tony to land the thing there and then.'

Lisa tensed her muscles. What was she letting herself in for? She had no intention of letting him treat her as he treated all the other women he plucked into his orbit, only to discard when he was tired of them.

She turned towards him, expecting to

see at the very least a taunting sense of fun. But what she saw was something quite different. It was a raw look of . . . of what?

With a jolt she realised it was the same look she used to see at Oxford, when she'd been certain it would only be a matter of days, hours, or even minutes before he told her that he loved her.

Only he never had. The kindness, the smooth talk and the flowers had meant nothing. He had misled her, deceived her, and she would never, ever forgive him for that.

She was nevertheless stunned by the look. She sat motionless on her seat. Forget it, she told herself. It's just his way with all women — as Monica had warned her from the start.

Catching her off her guard, Guy gathered her in his arms and lifted her out of the Cruiser, his face touching hers as he carried her to the shade of the trees.

His eyes searched her face. 'Yes,' he

said, kneeling down in front of her. 'You're even more beautiful now. Your shorter hair shows off your bone structure to perfection. Though the long hair was something else.'

He moved closer. 'I don't know how I used to stop myself running my fingers through it. I wish you'd grow it again.'

What was he talking about? He'd just rescued her from almost certain death and here he was talking about the length of her hair! One minute liking it short and the next wishing it was long again!

'My hair was a mess in those days,' she said, hardly believing that her hair could be the main topic of conversation after what they'd just been through.

If only he *had* run his fingers through her hair, she thought, biting her knuckles as she realised how crazily her thoughts were veering.

'No,' Guy said. 'It was never a mess. That was part of the trouble. You were so unaware of yourself. You were ... almost childlike in your freshness.

An unspoiled flower whose petals might be crushed by the slightest touch.'

She stared at him in amazement. He didn't normally use such poetic language but then this was probably what he said to all his girl friends. She shook her head. Forget it, Lisa. It's just words . . .

But it was his words that against her will transported her back more than five years to the night when he won first prize in the National Geographic photographic competition. He had turned towards her. She'd known by the slowness of the movement that he was no longer interested in what was happening at the meeting. She had lowered her eyes, for what she saw frightened her, yet excited her too. She had seen his arm moving slowly towards her, the hairs golden, as though lit by the sun. She had wanted to touch it.

'Come, Lisa,' he'd said. 'Let's go.'

Outside in the warm June air, he stopped. There was a look in his eyes she could not translate.

'It's late, Guy,' she said. 'I have work to do.'

'A coffee at my place, to round off the celebrations. It's not every day you win a trip to South America.'

Arriving at his flat her knees seemed to cave in under her. At last he's going to tell me he loves me, she thought.

At the front door he fumbled for the keys. She'd never been to his home before. In a trance she followed him in, as though chains binding her had been cut loose.

On the passage wall a photograph. A large portrait in black and white. Her own face against a shimmering background of leaves and sunlight sparkling on water.

'Like it?' Guy had asked, his arm sliding round her shoulder.

'Yes. But why is it up here?'

'I always mount my best photographs in prominent places,' he said. 'To remind me of the points I must remember.'

He carried the coffee to the lounge, slotted in a CD of slow guitar music. Turned off the main lights, leaving on one table lamp that lit up a small ivory carving of an elephant.

'What will you do when you get back from South America? Have you found a job yet?' It was the first time she'd dared to ask. This was his final term and she'd been hoping he'd be offered an engineering job in Oxford or somewhere nearby.

There was a moment of silence before he spoke. 'I may not come back,' he said. 'There's a chance I might get an assignment in South America with National Geographic. For one year,' he added quietly.

The news hit her like the backlash of a whip, knocking all reason from her mind. She mustered all her courage. Stood up. Held out her hand. 'Come on,' she said, her voice choking with emotion. 'Let's dance.'

'Well, well, well,' he'd said. 'What's got into my Lisa tonight?'

She smiled. Drifting towards him, she stroked the soft hair behind his neck, willing him to take her in his arms.

'This is no good, Lisa,' he said abruptly. 'I'll walk you home now otherwise you won't be able to get up tomorrow. But come round on Friday night next week. The night before I leave for Brazil. We can have a drink. Go out for a meal . . . '

'I don't want to go yet,' she said. 'Let's sit down and finish our coffee —'

He closed his eyes and breathed in deeply, in a way he often did. In a way she didn't understand.

Turning away from him she picked up the little ivory elephant on the table. Guy reached out and stroked it, his fingers touching hers. Together they gazed down at the hole where one tiny tusk was missing.

'This beautiful little creature was once part of an even more beautiful animal,' he said, in a voice she hardly recognised.

She stared at his arm, stretched out in front of her . . .

With a jolt she realised she was staring at his arms now. Strong, sunburned, torn and scratched from his headlong dash through the bush to save her from the elephants.

Dragging her eyes away, she stood up and dusted herself off. 'Well,' she said, 'I'd better start packing if I'm moving to Hippo Camp. Thank you for saving my life.'

'You were in danger. I was there. That's all there was to it, Lisa.' He raised his eyebrows. 'Come on. Let's have that smile again. Let's see those eyes sparkle. I always knew when you were really enjoying yourself — when your eyes sparkled. It used to make me want to hug you.'

Lisa kept her face as straight as she could, her lips puckering as she tried not to smile.

'And when you looked like that, I wanted to kiss you . . . '

And in that split second Lisa knew this was exactly what he was going to do.

Like a wave rolling up a beach she

felt the inevitability of a force that once unleashed would have no way of stopping . . .

The first touch lasted but a fleeting moment.

'Lisa,' he whispered.

Holding her at arms length he leaned back to look at her. She felt the blood rushing through her veins. She had a sudden urge to feel the velvet smoothness of his skin as she had so often dreamed of doing . . .

As though manipulated by a puppeteer her hands moved to his shoulders.

'I've missed you, Lisa,' he said.

She stared up at the leaves shimmering against the sky. She heard the screech of the cicadas, the cry of the fish eagle, the grunts of the hippos. This was no fantasy. No dream. This was for real . . .

But what was she thinking of? Guy Barrington only amused himself with a woman until he was tired of her, then discarded her for the next one. She'd seen her father do that all his life, seen her mother's short life of misery. She pulled away, wondering what on earth she had let herself in for.

Guy sat back on the dusty ground, his knees bent, his muscles tense and taut. 'Shall I pack for you before I go?' he asked softly.

'Thank you, but I can manage.' She needed time to herself. Time to work out in her own mind how she was going to cope with this new Guy. This new, liberated Lisa. This sudden new realisation that she was here, in this Eden of Central Africa with nothing to stop her enacting her wildest dreams, except . . .

She took several deep breaths. 'I'll see you later. Enoch will help me with the heavy stuff when he gets back from his village.'

As she turned away she noticed the gash on his chest was still bleeding. Without a word she ran to her tent and grabbed her first-aid tin. Ignoring Guy's protestations she cleaned the wound, applied antibiotic powder and covered it with a sterile dressing and strips of plaster, not once looking at his face or his arms.

'Thank you,' he said. 'I never realised you were so practical. You sure know your stuff.'

'Not really. All I know I learned from the World Wildlife team when we were here last year. They taught me everything about surviving in the bush. They even taught me how to stitch a wound. And when one of them was bitten by a snake they made me study the chart showing the patterns of the different snakes and the types of serum needed.'

'There's no end to your talents.' He smiled, then turned to go. 'I'll be back in a few hours.'

She watched him walk to the Land Cruiser. When he was half way he stopped, stood absolutely still, then started retracing his steps.

A few feet away from her he stopped again. His arms hung limply at his sides. His eyes were drawn together.

'Lisa?'

'Yes?'

'Do you ever . . . I mean . . . do you . . . ' He pressed his hands to the sides of his head and squeezed his eyes tightly closed as though he was trying to blot out something too painful to utter. Then he sighed and looked into her eyes.

'I'm sorry, Lisa, I don't know what made me do that. I don't know what came over me.'

She stared at him, unable to think of what to say. What a strange mixture he was. His parting words last night — What other reason could there be? And now this. Words that belied his actions.

'I'll retrieve your Land Rover tomorrow. I'll send it to Lusaka for repairs — if there's anything left of it.'

He turned and walked away without looking back, then drove off, clouds of dust billowing behind him.

⋆ ⋆ ⋆

By the time Guy returned, everything was ready to transport. His manner was relaxed and gave no hint of the tenseness that had gripped him a few hours ago. And whatever happened in the next few weeks, Lisa told herself firmly, no matter what he did, she had to control these involuntary responses of hers.

Not that there was any likelihood of a repetition. The kiss had clearly meant nothing. His cool, impersonal manner now was proof that she would indeed have been a fool if in those few moments of madness she had imagined it could be any other way.

But forewarned is forearmed. There's no way I'll let him lure me into making the same mistake twice.

When they'd loaded the last of her belongings he looked at her and grinned. 'You won't be sorry about this, Lisa. Without you I couldn't possibly finish the film.'

Lisa couldn't help smiling. 'I have no option,' she replied. 'My conscience wouldn't allow me to leave so important a mission in jeopardy.'

There *was* no other reason, she told herself firmly.

5

Lisa looked out over the wide ribbon of the river flowing past Hippo Camp. Enoch had erected her small green tent at the furthest end of the semi-circle of tents, a few feet from Guy's.

It felt good to be part of a community again. When Monica had given her the choice of working a project on her own or being part of a group, as she had been the previous year, she had jumped at the opportunity of doing original research without the direction of any other scientist. She was at the stage when, for her professional advancement, she needed to make an unaided contribution. But very soon she had felt the loneliness. Even paradise couldn't be complete, she had decided, without the occasional collaboration with one's colleagues.

She could hear Guy now, chatting to

Iliana. But just the tone and timbre of his deep baritone voice was enough to evoke memories she wished she could forget. She would have to stay as far away from him as possible, though she realised this would not be easy.

'When you've sorted out all your stuff, give us a shout, Lisa,' Guy said, appearing at the open flap of her tent. 'I'll give you a quick resume of what we've shot so far and what the broad plan is. There isn't a minute to lose.'

'I'll be as quick as I can,' Lisa said, pleased that they would be plunging into a work schedule straight away.

Guy's work tent was in the centre of the semi-circle of sleeping tents. The front and side flaps were rolled up, revealing a stunning view of the river with its teeming life of birds, crocodile and hippo. The back of the tent was piled with filmmaking paraphernalia, while in the middle stood a wooden trestle table and four chairs.

Lisa was relieved that Tony and Iliana were already there. Guy directed her to the chair on his right, with Iliana on his left.

After giving her a broad outline of the proposed structure of the film, he looked at her and smiled. 'But making a wildlife film is different from making any other kind of film. You have no rigid script to follow. You have a theme. You know what you want to say. You can't tell the animals what to do, so you have to know which aspects of their actions you need to capture. Once you have that raw material, it's in the cutting room that the film acquires a shape — like a sculptor who hacks a basic form from a piece of rock and must then carve in the detail. It's nothing before the editing and track laying are completed.'

'Guy, all that is true,' Iliana cut in. 'But without your shots there would be nothing. It is how *you* see the animals that makes you angle the camera the way you do and gives your films that unique quality — '

'No,' Guy said, shaking his head. 'My

camerawork is only part of it. We're a team, remember?' He turned back to Lisa. 'Right now I'm waiting for the rush reports on the exposed film I sent to my London studio last week. I don't even know if the exposure's right, or if there are any problems with the lenses. I rely heavily on rush reports to keep me in line technically — '

'Lisa, do not take any notice of all that technical stuff,' Iliana said. 'It means nothing!' She flashed Guy a smile. 'So how is it that your films are the best, *carino*?'

'Luck, probably,' Guy said, shrugging his shoulders. 'But with this one Lisa will guide my camera. She will establish the main thrust of this film.'

Iliana pursed her lips and looked at Lisa. 'And if you find him on his hands and knees most of the time,' she said slowly, 'it will *only* be because he likes to get down to ground level with his camera.'

In the pause that followed, Lisa thought she could detect something else that seemed to flow between Guy and Iliana, yet even though she knew that Iliana worshipped Guy, she began to wonder whether her feelings were reciprocated.

Guy took a deep breath and turned back to Lisa.

'You know, Lisa, it's an incredible coincidence that you chose to specialise in the elephant.'

She glanced at him sideways. 'Yes. It is,' she said, then quickly looked away in case her face betrayed her thoughts. Had he forgotten that it was he who'd led her to her single-minded line of study? That without him it would never have occurred? She could still remember every detail of what he'd said when she had picked up the little ivory elephant from his coffee table in Oxford, and how his words had moved her to tears . . .

'What an exquisite substance it is,' he'd said. 'Yet to many people the word *ivory* seems to have nothing at all to do with the word *elephant*. And why are the words *ebony* and *ivory* so often lumped together? Ivory is *alive!*' He had stroked the little elephant as though to resuscitate it. 'Part of an animal that once walked free in the wilderness. Using those tusks for feeding and playing and fighting and touching and loving . . .'

Lisa wiped the perspiration from her brow. She looked out at the wide swirling river. Clearly Guy had completely forgotten the incident.

She cleared her throat. 'First of all, I think it's absolutely vital to show how the loss through poaching of important family members has catastrophically affected the quality and behaviour of future offspring of each family group,' she said, hardly daring to look at Guy.

'And to show how ironic it is,' she carried on, 'that the output of ivory from the natural death of old elephants, which have large tusks, would have been no less, and might even have been more than that produced from the mass slaughter of young and middle aged animals, whose tusks are small and immature . . . '

As Lisa spoke Guy took notes, every now and then prompting her to expand her theories.

Tony was also scribbling furiously. 'I've already done the basic outline for the commentary,' he said, 'but now I think I'll do a complete re-write!' he told Guy excitedly.

'And I have another idea for the music,' Iliana said.

Guy raised a clenched fist and nodded. 'Sure. But we only have three weeks before we return to London for the post-production work. Iliana is recording the background noises,' he explained to Lisa. 'She'll help with the track laying in London — laying up all the different sounds, the music, the narration, which all have to be recorded then finally dubbed in.'

He touched Iliana's smooth olive-skinned arm. Lisa watched his fingers slide to the girl's elbow, then down again to her wrist. Does he do that with every woman he knows, she wondered? Or just those for whom he has a passing fancy?

'Iliana, I've been thinking about that music you've written, the tune you hummed to me the other night . . . ' He paused as the South American looked up at him, her mouth slightly open. 'It was . . . hauntingly beautiful. It would be exactly right for this new approach.'

Iliana clapped her hands together, her dark eyes wild with excitement as she leaned over and kissed Guy's cheek.

'The main theme could run through the film — reaching a crescendo in the final five minutes to tear at people's hearts . . . ' He half closed his eyes in exactly the way Lisa recalled whenever they had discussed something of exceptional beauty.

Then he looked down at his papers and his expression changed. 'But I regret that Xavier Orsino has already been offered a contract to write the music,' he said quietly. '*If* he signs the contract, it may be impossible to cancel. It's beyond my control, Iliana, but . . . don't give up hope yet. Orsino may turn it down.' He touched her arm again.

Iliana was silent, her face white with disappointment.

Guy shuffled his papers and put them into a neat pile.

'Lisa and I are going out for a couple of hours,' he said, abruptly pushing back his chair. 'We'll be back about six. We'll have another get-together before dinner.'

Lisa looked from Tony to Iliana. 'Aren't you two coming?'

'Too many people around when you're shooting a sequence is more hindrance than help,' Guy said, and Lisa knew that further protest would get her nowhere. Besides, he was probably right, as she already knew to her cost.

Stuffing her cameras and notebooks into her already bulging haversack, Lisa hurried to the Cruiser.

'Which way, Lisa?' Guy asked as they set off through the long dry grass.

★　★　★

Lisa guided him to the habitual grazing area of one of the herds she'd been studying. They were there in fifteen minutes, stopping only when a family of wart hog marched in single file across their path, their tails pointing stiffly upwards, their short legs moving like clockwork toys.

For the next two hours she orchestrated the sequences that Guy captured with his camera. Finally they pulled into a glade of ebony trees. Guy spread a rug on the ground close to the Cruiser. Relishing the relief of cool air beneath the umbrella of evergreen foliage, Lisa felt as though she was in a secret garden that only she and Guy had ever seen.

She handed him a tumbler of water. He took a sip, then turned towards her and smiled. 'It's as though we've been working together for years, isn't it, Lisa?'

Lisa didn't know where to look. She

nodded, then reached for the basket of sandwiches and tea Joseph had prepared. Anything to take her mind off the emotion his words evoked. From somewhere above them she heard the unmistakable song of a coucal, soft and muffled at first, getting louder and more plaintive, then fading into the sounds of the bush. It was a sound she would always remember. A sound that would remind her of this moment, however much she might try to forget it.

'What made you decide to make wildlife films?' she asked, searching the branches for a sight of the bird. 'I always thought photography was just your hobby.'

He snapped a small twig from a branch above his head. 'Do you really need to ask me that?'

Lisa shrugged. 'Well, I know winning the National Geographic prize must have triggered it off, but — you're an engineer — '

'Nothing in the world of engineering

persuaded me to spend the rest of my life pursuing it. It would have been as stifling as my career in Law was.'

'So . . . ?'

'Well? Don't you remember, Lisa?'

'No,' she answered, shaking her head.

'Of course you do! It was you who fired me up with that incredible single-minded passion of yours — '

Lisa laughed. 'Are you sure you're remembering the right person?'

'I'd see the rapture on your face when you spoke of your work — just like I've seen it today. And I thought that whatever it was that turned you on like that must be worthwhile looking at. It was you, Lisa. You did it — '

'Yes, but . . . but my love of elephants was because of you! You made me aware of their plight. Don't you remember that little carving you had?'

Lisa bit her lip. She saw his far-away expression. How stupid to have brought that up, but before she could stop herself the words were out.

'With one tusk missing?' he asked.

She nodded.

He dragged his fingers across his chin, leaving white marks on his sunburned skin.

'I remember very well,' he said.

Lisa felt as though the space between them had come alive with tendrils that drew her towards Guy. She swung away from him, but it was no good. The years had been bridged, locking them in a time warp and kindling the same fire that all those years ago had almost burned out of control . . .

The tiny elephant had been like a chain linking not only their hands but their minds as well. Until then no one had motivated her to care about what happened to children or old people — or even animals, in spite of her studying zoology. This new awareness had overwhelmed her. It was a new dimension in her passion-starved life. She had felt closer to him in mind than she had ever felt to anyone, and had wanted that safe feeling to last forever.

When the little elephant had clattered to the ground they did not pick it up. Sliding his hands to the tops of her arms he had slowly drawn her towards him. His breath had roared in her ear, like waves crashing on rocks . . .

Lisa sat rigidly on the edge of the rug. Two giraffes ambled through the trees close by, but she barely saw them.

'Lisa. What have I done to make you so on edge? You never used to be so touchy. Am I expecting too much from you? Or perhaps you just aren't up to this heat?'

She whisked a fly off her leg then stood up and walked blindly into the bush.

'Lisa! Come back!'

She stopped, then turned and moved a few token paces towards him.

I can't let him guess what I've remembered . . .

'Just give me a few moments,' she said.

So many memories were being brought to life by his presence. It had been madness to allow a situation to arise that would lead them down the same path they had travelled five years ago, when she'd been powerless to control her overwhelming need for him.

He had made the world a new and wonderful place. Nobody had made her feel wanted before. Nobody had cared whether she was there or not . . .

'Lisa!'

Taking a deep breath she resumed walking back to the car. 'I don't know what's wrong with me,' she said. 'Maybe you're right. This heat seems to have given me a headache.'

He took her arm and helped her into the Cruiser, then started up the engine. 'You should have mentioned your headache sooner. One can't afford to get ill on a job like this, with no proper hospital for hundreds of miles and only a bush clinic for emergencies — '

'Guy, it's only a headache. Really, I've had much worse.'

Lisa was furious with herself for her ridiculous behaviour. She didn't want him or any other man. They were all the same. Just like her father. So why this nonsense?

Yet she was finding it difficult to reconcile Guy's betrayal five years ago with the man sitting next to her now. He seemed so different from the picture she'd harboured all these years.

★ ★ ★

On Guy's insistence the evening meeting was postponed until after dinner to give Lisa a chance to rest.

'I want Lisa to pinpoint the most important issues,' he said when they were all gathered together in Guy's work tent.

There was an awkward silence as they all waited for Lisa to speak. She heard the generator splutter. The lights flickered, making their shadows on the sides of the tent look as though they were moving, yet no one had moved an inch.

Guy cleared his throat. 'So, Lisa. What next?'

Lisa felt a surge of excitement, as she suddenly became aware of how important her contribution to the film could be. She looked at Guy, saw the anticipation on his face and wondered how she could ever have wavered in her decision to join his team.

'A few days ago I followed a herd across the river to the Chilongola woodlands, where I did a lot of my research last year. They're eating their way through the trees there, but will soon be moving on to forests further afield. Two young cows are heavily pregnant — '

She gave Guy a guilty look to remind him of how sorry she was to have ruined his previous shots. 'We might be lucky to witness one of the births. But more important, there are orphans in that group who are missing out on parental guidance. Delinquents, you could call them. I know roughly where to find the herd — '

'That's settled, then,' Guy declared. 'We'll leave tomorrow morning before breakfast. No, we'll take the helicopter to save time. You could drive over to Longu tonight, Tony, be airborne at dawn and pick us up here by six. With Lisa's help we'll get far more of the kind of footage we need in a shorter period of time. The deadline is closer than we think, so let's call it a day now and get some sleep.'

Guy's hand lingered on Lisa's shoulder as he pulled her chair back for her. She almost wished he were rude and thoughtless. She wished she could hate him the way he deserved to be hated.

'Sleep well, Lisa,' he said softly.

But the unaccustomed noise of the generator made sure that Lisa did not sleep. It was even worse when the generator stopped promptly at ten o'clock, plunging the entire camp into darkness. As the lights went out in her tent, and the fan was silenced, the night noises intensified. She could hear the whoop of the night owl and the grunts of the grazing hippos, and the faint crackling of the night fire near her tent.

She watched the shadows of the flames flickering on the canvas. Guy was in the tent next to hers. Could he see the shadows too? Was he remembering, she wondered? Or was he only concerned with the film and its success?

She buried her head in the pillow, trying to blot out his image, willing him to leave her in peace. She pulled her knees up, put her hands over her ears and closed her eyes tightly.

But with each flicker of the flames his image intruded further, until it seemed to her that she was no longer in a tent in the middle of Africa, but back as a first year undergraduate at Oxford University . . .

6

It is an unseasonably warm day in Oxford for late April, with a hint of early summer in the air. The OU Photographic Society is holding one of its colour slide exhibitions. Guy is sitting next to her. In the glow of the projector she becomes aware that he is tense. Instead of looking at the screen, he is looking at her, as he so often does.

All of a sudden he stands up. 'Let's go,' he whispers, and without waiting for her to answer he leads her out to the forecourt.

'Well, where to now, Lisa?' he asks.

His voice is gruff. A muscle twitches in his cheek. She wonders what has become of his usual relaxed manner.

'The pub?' she says, shrugging her shoulders, because isn't that where they always go after the PS meetings?

Guy chooses a table in a quiet,

low-ceilinged room away from the bar. He disappears for a few minutes and comes back with the drinks. The regular crowd hasn't arrived yet and she is conscious that for the first time ever, they are alone.

He sits close to her on the bench against the wall. He is strangely restive.

'You've never told me anything about yourself, Lisa. Your childhood — '

'I've had a very dull, uneventful life,' she says.

'I can hardly believe that. An attractive, intelligent girl like you?'

A warm flush invades her cheeks. She wishes she could be like the other students, who would laugh and make some sophisticated remark to put him in his place and make everyone else laugh too.

His hand reaches up. With cool fingers he pushes a long strand of hair from her forehead. 'Sorry,' he says. 'I couldn't resist doing that.'

She takes a sip of her orange juice. She should have some witty reply but nothing comes into her head. Instead, she says, boldly, 'But what about you? I'm sure you must have led a very interesting life.' According to Monica he is about fifteen years older than she is, so he must be thirty-three at least. She wishes she had the courage to ask what had gone wrong with his marriage and why his baby had died. And why it is that he is still at university. And where he goes on those weekends when he disappears without telling anyone where he is going.

He laughs. 'My past is a closed book, I'm afraid, but I'm not a perpetual student, if that's what you're thinking. Though this *is* my second time around.'

'How come?' she asks. She hopes he will not think she is too inquisitive.

'My father made me follow in his legal footsteps, but I hated the rat race of the city. When I had some money behind me, I came back here — for my sins.' He is speaking in a soft monotone and she has a feeling there is far more to it than that.

'But why civil engineering?'

He takes a big gulp of his beer. 'Not sure really. After the death of my son . . . ' He shuts his eyes tightly, then slowly opens them again.

He pauses. Breathes deeply. His nostrils flare. Lisa can sense the effort he is making to carry on. 'I wanted to make a fresh start,' he says at last. 'Do something creative — to — '

She feels a lump in her throat. He has never spoken of his baby son before. She longs to comfort him, to encourage him to expound but is too afraid to probe.

He picks up his mug of beer. 'I've an idea, Lisa.' Suddenly his voice is light and bright again. 'I've just thought of the perfect place to solve your problems of contrasting light. Have you ever been punting on the river?'

She shakes her head.

'In this fantastic spring weather it's a must. Deep shadows. Light filtering through the leaves. Reflections on the water . . . ' His lips are slightly parted.

'Please, come with me on Sunday — '

Without warning, the crowd from the Photographic Society spill into the room, laughing and shouting.

'Oh, so this is where you two disappeared to!' Monica says, squeezing onto the bench beside Lisa and giving her a knowing look. 'Be careful,' she whispers when Guy goes for more drinks. 'And don't say I didn't warn you.'

Lisa shrugs. 'Don't worry, Monica. He's only interested in me because of my camera. He treats me almost as though I were his daughter or his niece — '

'He's very proud of you,' Monica says. 'Every good photograph you take is an achievement for him too.'

'It's the first time someone's done anything like this for me, bothered about what I do. So it makes me want to please him all the more — '

'You're even losing your shyness,' Monica says. 'Shhh! Here he comes . . . '

Lisa opened her eyes, rubbing them as if to obliterate the tide of memories which every day were flooding her consciousness, haphazardly, darting without warning from one vivid recollection to another, with no chronological sequence.

Jumping out of bed she unzipped the flap of her tent and sat down on her little stool to watch the sky. In a few minutes it would begin to change from black to pearly grey to brilliant blue — a rapid transformation you could only see in the tropics and which never ceased to delight her.

In no time a faint glimmer of light silvered the river. Hippos snorted as they plopped back into the water, and the sky became alive with birds.

She peered at the luminous dial of her watch. There was just time to shower and dress and be ready to leave at six.

As she stood in the stream of tepid water, she thought about the day ahead.

It was essential to remain positive and single minded about the task ahead. I must adopt a totally professional attitude at all times, she told herself. I have an important job to do. There is no time for anything else.

Dressing in her usual khaki shorts and shirt, she gathered up her sun hat and haversack and made her way towards the tantalising smell of coffee. Any minute now Tony would be arriving in the helicopter, so Lisa was surprised when at that moment he zoomed into camp — in the Land Cruiser.

'Don't blame me — ' Tony shouted, striding towards Guy as if to buffet the onslaught he was certain he would get.

Lisa looked at the granite expression on Guy's face, glad that she wasn't in Tony's shoes.

'Where's the helicopter?' Guy demanded.

'They've run out of aviation fuel — '

Guy pressed his fingers into the top of his head. 'This will cost us many precious hours. Perhaps days!' He sighed, letting out his breath until his face sagged with the futility of trying to overcome the difficulties of working miles from civilisation. Then, as though a cloud had lifted from his head he raised his chin and focused on each one of them in turn. 'Okay,' he said, his eyes narrowing with determination. 'We have no option now. We'll take the new long-wheel base Land Rover. More reliable than the Cruiser and better equipped for emergencies, though less comfortable. And there'll only be room for Lisa and me and the equipment, I'm afraid.'

'It's a pity my beautiful new vehicle is a wreck,' Lisa said lamely.

'Well, you can forget that. It won't be ready for weeks. Come on,' he urged. 'Let's get on the road.'

* * *

The bush seemed more alive with activity than Lisa had ever seen it. Monkeys leapt like acrobats from tree to tree, while brightly coloured birds in their thousands heralded the day with their symphony of song. Like one big happy family, herds of zebra, wildebeest and giraffe drifted towards the river for their early morning drink, quite unconcerned as Guy and Lisa drove through their midst. Less brazen was a small herd of buffalo, which retreated in a flurry of dust as the Land Rover approached.

'We're almost at the turn-off for the pontoon,' Lisa said, holding on to the seat as they skidded round a sharp bend in the narrow twisting track.

Suddenly a lone bull elephant appeared like a mountain in front of them, his grey shape camouflaged in the dappled shade of the trees.

As Guy slammed on the brakes the massive beast spread his ears and lifted his head high, then blew down through his trunk. He gave a sharp shake of his head and let out a shrill trumpet as he lumbered towards the Land Rover.

Guy jerked the gear lever into reverse.

Lisa hit the dashboard as the vehicle zigzagged backwards. Guy swung the wheel and crashed through a narrow gap in the trees, throwing her sideways.

'Where's your seat belt?' he yelled as a swirling cloud of dust enveloped them. 'Do you want to get killed?'

Through the dust Lisa could see the elephant right behind them. He was no more than a teenager by the size of his tusks, but must weigh at least ten thousand pounds. He could easily flatten them in the foul mood he was in.

But suddenly he waved his trunk and veered off into the trees. Guy manoeuvred the Land Rover back onto the track and after a few hundred yards he stopped, leaving the engine running.

'Are you all right?' he asked, moving towards her and peering up into her face.

'I'm fine,' she said, keeping her eyes level.

'That was pretty close. I wonder why he was so aggressive?'

Lisa edged away from his arm.

'That's what the presence of poachers does to a gentle, peaceful animal,' she said. 'You'd be aggressive too if you'd lost your uncle, brother, father, mother, aunt, sister — '

'Or your girl friend,' Guy said quietly.

Lisa froze.

Slowly she turned her head. Apart from his eyebrows, which lifted slightly as she met his gaze, he was sitting absolutely still.

Lisa's hands tightened into fists.

'The slaughter of so many young elephants has changed their social life,' she went on, knowing she had to keep talking even though she could hear her own voice becoming faster and more highly pitched by the second, like the commentator at a race meeting. 'It'll be a long time before these changes stop having a serious effect on their behavioural patterns and on their natural breeding — '

'I'm sure you're right,' Guy murmured, slowly sliding his arm from the back of the seat down to Lisa's shoulder.

'*Guy! Over there!*' she yelled, instinctively grabbing his arm as she pointed to the group of teenage bachelors loping through the trees towards them, their trunks in the air and their ears out wide.

Guy took one look at their steady advance and put his foot down on the accelerator. Lisa glanced at his face. She saw no trace of fear, but the steely look of someone who knew that caution was more important than bravado.

Only when they reached the banks of the river did he slow down.

'They all seem to be in a fighting mood today,' he said, still watching the track behind them.

But Lisa was staring at the pontoon lying immobile on the other side of the river. 'I hope it'll come soon,' she said, looking nervously around her.

Guy waited a few minutes, then pressed the horn.

'We could be here all day,' he said

when there was still no response from the men milling around on the pontoon.

Lisa adjusted her binoculars. 'Guy, I don't think that pontoon's working at all. Maybe they're repairing it. It certainly needed it last week — '

'It looks fine,' Guy said crossly. He pressed the horn again.

This time the men responded.

'Come back in two days,' they shouted.

Guy shouted back, insisting that he had to cross immediately. Finally, after much yelling and gesticulating, the men agreed and started hauling on the pulley ropes.

'They could have done that straight away, instead of messing us around,' he muttered as he started up the engine and eased the Land Rover onto the rickety craft. 'Stand in the middle, Lisa,' he said, frowning as the murky water splashed over the edges of the fragile floor.

With a face like thunder he pointed

out the weak, fraying bits of the pulley to Lisa.

'You wouldn't have a hope in this current,' he said. 'If one of those snapped.'

Lisa sighed with relief when they reached the other side and the Land Rover safely bounced down on to the flimsy planks of wood bridging the pontoon to the muddy bank.

'I'm sorry, Guy. I'm really sorry. I just never thought about the safety of the equipment — '

'Do you think I care about *that*?' Guy said, swerving left and pulling in under a tree fifty yards up the bank. 'Do you think I would have risked your life if I'd known just how dangerous that crossing would be?' His lips were drawn tightly across his teeth. 'I don't suppose you noticed, but half-way across, that thing almost fell apart!'

'Oh, no!' She swallowed hard.

'Oh, yes! And there's no way we're crossing on *that* pontoon again!'

Lisa felt a tide of frustration rise up

in her chest. Everything seemed to be going wrong. Perhaps her suggestion to film in the Chilongola woodlands had been made too hastily.

'We could ask the pontoon men the best way to the Chombo Bridge,' she suggested, doing her best to smile. 'It's miles away but may be our only hope.'

Guy nodded briefly then without another word he opened the door and began striding down the rocky slope to the river.

Lisa jumped down onto the stony ground and watched him, feeling the tension rise with each aggressive step he took. When he came back he looked like someone about to commit a murder.

'You won't believe this, Lisa. But your precious Chombo Bridge collapsed last rainy season and nobody, but *nobody* has even *begun* to repair it.'

'But that's the only bridge for hundreds of miles!'

Guy kicked a stone and watched it hurtle down the slope. 'Oh well,' he said, hurrying Lisa back into the Land

Rover. 'I suppose we're lucky the pontoon repairs will be completed by four o'clock tomorrow afternoon. They've promised to work around the clock. I'll send a radio message to Tony,' he added, and reached for the short-wave equipment on the dashboard.

'But there's no rest-house on this side of the river . . . '

'Count yourself lucky we've a good supply of water and petrol, my girl. And if we're careful there's enough food in these cold-boxes for several days. We've even got a futon rolled up under the back seat. And a couple of pillows.'

Lisa fastened her seat belt, but said nothing.

'What's wrong, Lisa?' he asked, grinning broadly in a way that immediately put her on her guard. 'You're not afraid, are you?'

Without moving her head she flicked her eyes at him, then quickly looked away.

'Come on, then,' he said. 'We're wasting valuable time. Let's get moving. It won't hurt us to spend one night in the Land Rover. There's even a mosquito net . . . '

* * *

Following the tyre marks she and Enoch had so recently made, Lisa kept her eyes on the track in front of her, all thoughts of the night ahead vanishing as she revelled in the sights and sounds and smells of the unspoilt bush.

'Look!' she said, her excitement rising as the familiar terrain unfolded before them. 'There's the huge baobab tree we camped next to last year, right on the edge of the escarpment! We're nearly there. The dambo is just north of here.'

Guy nodded, smiling at her enthusiasm. As the ground dipped, the waterhole came into view, shimmering like an oasis in the morning sun.

'This way, Guy. We could park at pretty close range. We used a similar vehicle last year, so I don't think there'll be any trouble.'

At first glance there were at least thirty female elephants. Some were ripping branches off trees, some having dust baths while others were drinking or wallowing in the muddy water.

Guy inched cautiously forward. None of them took any notice of the Land Rover so he parked and quickly unpacked his cameras.

'This is amazing,' he said, giving Lisa's arm a squeeze as she guided him to a family group she had previously studied.

While he was concentrating on a cluster of young females who had drifted to the other side of the dambo, Lisa saw that another group was advancing from the left. Something about their demeanour made her spine prickle. It might only be idle interest, she thought, but after their earlier experience . . .

Should she alert Guy?

Before she could jump into the driver's seat, the new group of elephants had formed a classic defensive circle. Her eyes flew to Guy. He was facing away from the circle, quite oblivious of the possible threat. It would be risky to alert him now, though she was fairly sure the elephants would remain wary only until they too had weighed up the unfamiliar vehicle.

As if at a signal they began to flap their ears and shake their heads — pretty harmless movements, but at any moment their mood could change.

Lisa held her breath. A rivulet of sweat trickled down her spine. The only thing to do was to sit tight.

Then, to another indiscernible signal, the elephants quietly abandoned their defensive stance. Lisa breathed out.

Guy was safe.

★ ★ ★

Disappointingly there was still no sign of the two pregnant cows. Guy spent the afternoon shooting sequences of the family groups Lisa recognised, while she took her own backup shots, focusing on the trunks and outer markings of the ears, establishing without doubt their identity. Working at breakneck speed she recorded ages, behaviour and relationship to other members of the family. Both she and Guy were totally absorbed in their work until the light began to fade and they were suddenly fighting off an army of flying insects.

'Have you seen the time, Lisa?' Guy said, whacking a moth from his neck as he began packing away the equipment.

'Time always flies when you're busy,' she said, as they drove up the gently sloping bank and headed for the giant baobab tree.

'Or enjoying yourself,' he said.

★　★　★

'Come and look at this, Lisa. Pure primeval wilderness. Unequalled any-where in the world.' With a sweep of his hands Guy indicated the endless vista of bush and distant blue hills fading into the horizon beyond the steep escarpment.

Lisa shivered as she stood beside him. Through the trees, water tinkled over rocks. They were not far from an ox-bow bend in the river, which swung eastwards, cascading in a miniature waterfall into the open plain below. This was one of those unique moments, she thought. A moment that would be frozen in time to bring back when all this was over and they had both gone their separate ways again.

'It's like a Garden of Eden,' she said.

Guy turned to face her. 'We're so lucky to be here, Lisa . . . '

She knew that tone. Knew it had little to do with the job they had come here to do. Nothing to do with the filming. And nothing at all to do with the idyllic surroundings.

She walked a few more steps to the edge of the escarpment. The colour of the sky had deepened from peach to burnt orange. Soon it would be dark, and what then, she wondered?

Guy walked slowly towards her. 'If we have our meal now we'll have the rest of the evening to relax.'

Lisa stopped breathing. Since dusk had stopped their work, she had felt the tension build between them.

He touched her shoulder. 'Or should I have asked if you have any other plans?'

'I have my notes to complete — '

'Oh come on, Lisa.' Gently he held her arm. 'We don't have a lot of spare time and it seems a pity to — '

Lisa edged out of his grip. 'You're in charge,' she said quietly. 'Please just do what you think is right. I'm here to get this film finished and if we have to work right through the night that's okay with me too. We're not on holiday and we can't stay here indefinitely because there's not enough food and I know what your appetite's like so let's just get on with it and forget the niceties — '

'Lisa! What's wrong? You've changed — '

'You're the one who's changed,' she said, trying desperately to remain calm, knowing that she was overacting to the situation. 'Anyway, it's pointless comparing any changes that may or may not have taken place.' She walked away so that he could no longer see her eyes.

He followed her. 'You have a short memory, Lisa.'

'Short? You call five years short?'

She bit her lip and squeezed her eyes shut. But it was too late. For the hundredth time she saw herself careering out of his flat and fleeing to her hideout in the Welsh mountains where Monica had finally tracked her down and made her come to her senses.

Guy moved another step towards her, grasped her arms and turned her round to face him. 'You can't wipe out what happened in the past. It's real. It's still with us. Here!' He prodded his chest with his finger. 'Besides, Lisa, you can't let go of the past without facing it again.'

Lisa quivered with indecision. Should she confront him now, as she should have done five years ago instead of running away? Get it off her chest? Release herself from the invasive memories for once and all? Memories that were driving her mad.

But she didn't want his sympathy. And what good would it do to expose the wounds?

'Come on,' she said, marching away from him, hauling the folding chairs out of the Land Rover and slamming them down on the ground several feet apart. 'Let's finish the unpacking. Soon this'll all be over and we can pretend we never met again. Because obviously we weren't meant to.'

Without a word Guy cleared everything from the back of the Land Rover and stacked it neatly at the base of the baobab tree. Dragging his fingers down the side of his face, he looked upwards and let out a long deep sigh. For a few moments he gazed at the swiftly darkening panorama, then wandered off to gather twigs and dry logs for their campfire. In the ensuing silence Lisa unpacked the picnic Joseph had prepared.

'There's enough left for tomorrow's lunch,' Guy said when they'd finished eating.

Getting no response he tossed another log onto the fire.

Lisa watched the sparks rise into the black of the night. She knew she should be happy. She wanted to be happy. She was here in this Garden of Eden, helping to make one of the most important films of Guy Barrington's career . . . helping to save the elephant . . .

Guy handed her a mug of steaming coffee.

'Thanks,' she said, keeping her eyes on the sparks shooting from the log into the black of the night.

'Lisa . . . ' His voice was low, barely audible.

Lisa clutched the mug until she thought it would crack into a thousand pieces in her hand. 'Yes?'

'Why did you do it?'

'Do what?'

'Need you ask?'

'I don't know what you mean.'

'You could at least have telephoned. Or written. I tried to find you. Nobody knew where you'd gone.'

She would never forget climbing those stairs. He could have all the women he wanted, but she wasn't going to be one of them, waiting in line for her turn. She'd been alone all her life so she could carry on the same way.

She'd seen enough of her father's string of women to know that even if everything looked wonderful one day, tomorrow there'd be someone else. Well, that kind of life was not for her. She was lucky she'd acted decisively. If not, she'd have been just one more in a long line of hopefuls, eating their hearts out for the crumbs, like poor Iliana . . .

She repeated in her head the maxim she had composed for herself during those weeks on her own in the Brecon Beacons.

If you don't want to be hurt then don't get involved. On your own you're safe. Nobody can let you down . . .

'Lisa, don't pretend to be the innocent. You know what you did. And you sure pulled the wool over my eyes.'

Her mouth dropped open. 'You're crazy!' she blurted out. 'I did nothing of the sort!' She thrust her head in her hands. 'Oh, what does it matter now? How you must all have laughed at me. I bet it was one big joke — another conquest for Barrington!'

Lisa drew in her breath as she realised that her voice sounded as though it belonged to someone else — harsh and bitter, and full of hatred. An alien sound that she didn't like and wished she could retract.

Guy scratched the top of head, then jumped up and walked quickly to the trunk of the tree. He threw open one of the cool-boxes and brought out two tins of cold beer. When he came back he moved his chair until it was almost touching Lisa's.

He snapped open the tins, handed one to Lisa and sat down beside her.

The faint sound of distant drums drifted across the escarpment, throbbing through her body as her heart began to pound to its rhythm.

'Look at me, Lisa!' he said. 'You and I have to talk.'

7

Lisa waited for him to speak. They had already spent several hours talking about the film so what could he possibly want to talk about now? One thing was certain. It definitely wouldn't be about the elephants. Not the way he was looking at her now.

She took a gulp from the can of beer, recoiling at the bitter taste. She thought of the long night stretching ahead of them. Almost twelve hours of darkness, lit only by the stars and the moon and the glow of the fire. Already the atmosphere was tense. What would it be like in another few hours?

Out of the corner of her eye she traced the outline of his body as he sat motionless in front of her. She had once loved him as she had never loved another human being. Had this only been because he was the first person to show any interest in her welfare? Was that all it had been? Gratitude? Gratitude for his kindness to her? For years she had tried to rationalise her behaviour, but now in the stillness of the African night she began to wonder . . .

Stop! she told herself. You're going to let it happen again, aren't you? But you know that kindness doesn't cancel out betrayal . . .

At last he moved.

With one finger of his right hand he gently pulled her chin round so that she was forced to look at him. She jerked away. He was a touching person. Once she had thought he cared because nobody had ever touched her in that casual, gentle way before. Now she knew it had meant nothing. Guy touched everybody, just as elephants are always touching each other with their trunks. He was just that kind of person.

'Lisa! What's wrong with you? You look as though you've seen a snake. I'm not going to bite you.'

'Okay,' she said, doing her best to blank her mind of all her negative thoughts. 'So what did you want to talk about?'

'Everything, Lisa. You and me — '

'There's nothing personal to talk about, Guy. You see, I'm not in the queue any more.'

'*Queue?*' He laughed out loud, then his voice dropped to a whisper. 'I should be so lucky — '

Lisa was taken aback by the bitterness of his tone. She was puzzled by the look of indecision she saw in his eyes, as though there was something of great importance on his mind and he was trying to decide whether or not to tell her what it was.

'Oh, come on, Guy,' she said. 'Isn't that how it's always been?'

Guy wrestled with his conscience. He leaned back on his arms, stretching his legs in front of him as he watched the flames of the fire reflecting on her face, highlighting the contours that for so many years had remained vivid in his mind. Contours he'd imagined running his fingers over more times than he could remember. Why didn't he tell her now? She deserved to know.

Surely it wasn't too late. If only he'd told her right at the beginning, when he first met her, but somehow the right moment had never presented itself. Or had he been too afraid to lose her altogether?

He counted to ten. It was now or never. But he would have to ease her into it slowly. Perhaps if he told her just enough to explain the anomalies of his behaviour, it might end this impasse between them.

'What about *us*, Lisa?' he blurted out. 'The feelings we have for each other?'

Be careful, he told himself when he saw the look on her face, conscious more than ever of the need for circumspect, yet desperate to know if there was any hope.

'*What* feelings?' she asked slowly.

'Stop pretending, will you, Lisa. Surely — '

'No, Guy. Surely nothing. Any feelings we may have had for each other died a long time ago. And you can't pretend they were worth preserving, anyway.'

Guy shook his head. He thought he knew Lisa. He couldn't have been so wrong.

'Why the barrier, Lisa? You know that isn't true. I *know* it isn't true. My memory happens to be very good.'

'What's the point of remembering something that had no meaning then, so couldn't possibly mean anything now.'

'What are you fighting, Lisa?'

'Look, can we drop this subject, please.'

He stood up and looked down at her. 'How can we, Lisa? It's here. Between us. Around us. Can't you feel it? It *exists!*'

'Only in your imagination,' she said, avoiding his gaze.

'Lisa, please, look at me.'

Slowly she turned her head.

'You don't have a very high opinion of me, do you?'

Lisa clenched her teeth, only just stopping herself from telling him that the way he conducted his personal life seemed not unlike her father's, and that was something she could not tolerate. 'I never said that, Guy. I greatly admire your undisputed brilliance in the art of film-making, but . . . '

'But what, Lisa?'

'Oh, what's the point. Why dredge up old history. What's done is done. I'm not a part of your life. We've only been thrown together like this because we both believe passionately in the need to save the elephant. Many people might not understand this dedication and love. But we do. And that's all we have in common.'

Guy dragged his fingers through his hair, then smoothed it down with his palm as he realised the moment was fast slipping away. 'So that's how you feel, is it?'

'I know you feel the same way,' she said. 'And it's this compassion that sets your films apart from other people's.'

He knew she had deliberately misinterpreted his question, but decided to let it go.

'I also insist on perfection from my team, and that's one reason why you're here now. Although it's not the only one,' he muttered, catching his breath as he willed himself to curb his tongue. Now was clearly not the time to tell her. She would have to be receptive otherwise there'd be a danger that she would misinterpret his words and think that he was making excuses. After that there might never be another chance. 'Your input will give the film scientific credibility — '

Suddenly he lifted his hands and shook his head. 'Why the hell are we talking about *films*? What have *films* got to do with *you* and *me*?'

Lisa turned away from the fire so that Guy would not see the flush she felt spreading across her face.

She heard him move towards her, twigs crackling beneath his feet. Unable to stop herself she turned again to face him. His eyes, lit by the glow of the fire were wide and staring. His arms hung loosely at his sides but there was a tenseness about him that made Lisa certain that they wouldn't stay there much longer.

'Don't touch me!' she said, hurrying to the Land Rover. As she scrambled into the front seat she felt decidedly foolish for overreacting to something that may not even have happened. 'I must get some sleep,' she said.

'No problem,' he replied lightly, resting his elbows on the rim of the open window and briefly closing his eyes. 'Without all the equipment, the rear of the vehicle is more than wide enough for us both on the futon.'

Lisa glanced at the narrow space behind her. 'You're welcome to it all. I'll be quite happy here on the front seat.'

'Oh no you won't! Not unless you

want to get gnawed to pieces by mosquitoes.'

'I must have been bitten already. A few more won't matter.'

'No you weren't,' he said gently. 'Not with four coils burning.'

Lisa realised now what the pungent smell near the fire had been. 'How thoughtful of you,' she said.

He nodded and smiled. 'This vehicle is equipped with almost everything one needs in the bush. And it has a nifty mosquito net that hooks onto the roof with Velcro. We can't be too careful. I was told that malaria is far more prevalent here than it used to be.'

'I've taken my weekly malaria pill religiously.'

'But they don't guarantee a hundred percent protection, do they, Lisa? So don't argue. You will sleep on the futon. And so will I.'

'But — '

'And I promise no harm will come to you.'

Lisa was surprised to detect no

sarcasm in his voice. But how unnerving that even though she wasn't looking at him, she knew that he was smiling.

* * *

Lisa lay quite still, every muscle in her body as taut as a string on a hunter's bow. It was hard to believe that this was happening at all. She told herself the only reason she was here in this bizarre situation was because of the professional interest Guy had in her expertise, but that didn't make it any easier.

'Are you comfortable, Lisa?'

She pressed herself as far as she could against the side of the Land Rover so that her knees touched the cool metal. 'Yes,' she answered. 'Are you okay?'

'I'm fine, but you can move back a little if you like. I have more than my fair share of space.'

'I'm quite comfortable, thank you,' she said.

'Pleasant dreams, Lisa.'

She heard him settle onto his pillow. She made her breathing sound as even as possible. If he thought she was asleep he would probably sleep too. But how could she relax when she could feel his breath on the back of her neck and smell the wood smoke on his skin?

The heat in the Land Rover was building up. The tucked-in net made her feel as if she was imprisoned in a cage. In a desperate attempt to relax she clenched her fists into tight balls, the method she'd used when studying for her finals. Tighten every muscle one by one, then let go and feel as though you're sinking through the mattress.

She tried it now. Slowly the tension ebbed from her body. If she could just maintain this floating sensation she was sure sleep would come soon . . .

A languorous calm began to overtake her. But when she felt Guy's tenuous touch she saw a light flash before her eyes as though all at once a thousand candles had been lit.

First his fingers touched her cheek,

then they moved to her hair.

She turned to face him. '*Oh, Guy . . .* '

'Lisa? Are you all right? What is it?'

With a start she opened her eyes. A gibbous moon had risen low in the sky, throwing its muted light upon them both. Only a few inches separated them, but he was facing the other way with his head twisted back to look at her, his eyes half closed with sleep. His hands were nowhere near her.

'Nothing,' she managed to say.

'I could have sworn I heard you call my name,' he said sleepily. 'I must have been dreaming. Go back to sleep. I'm sorry I woke you.'

'I'm sorry too,' she answered, thankful for the semi-darkness that masked her burning cheeks.

It was hard to believe it had been a dream, for she was certain she could still feel his fingers on her face. 'I sometimes have vivid dreams when I'm too hot,' she said, thankful for the genuine excuse.

She turned over and closed her eyes, inching herself closer to the edge of the vehicle so that she missed seeing the little smile that crept over Guy's lips, and the lift of his eyebrows. She also missed seeing his hand, which moved as though to caress her in a gesture of reassurance, but which he withdrew a moment before his fingers reached her arm.

* * *

Through half open eyes Lisa watched the dawn leach the darkness from the sky.

There was no sign of Guy but she heard clattering noises and could smell fresh wood smoke drifting through the mosquito net. Running her hands down the back of her legs to ease the tension of maintaining the same position for so long, she sat up just as the first rays of the sun filtered through the dry yellow grass.

Guy's voice alongside the Land Rover made her jump.

'It wasn't the way you thought, you know, Lisa.'

She stifled a yawn. 'What wasn't the way I thought?'

'The way things turned out on that last night. When we'd planned to have a quiet evening together . . . just the two of us . . . '

The last thing Lisa wanted was for him to feel obliged to make up some paltry excuse in the hope that he could make up for his actions with sweet talk. She knew now that she should have confronted him at the time, asked him what he thought he was doing. But she'd been too distraught to think logically, and now it was far, far too late.

'It doesn't matter now,' she said.

'Oh, but it does, Lisa, don't go . . . No — please listen . . . '

But Lisa had dragged the net aside and was already marching off towards the stream.

When she returned from washing, Guy had buttered two rolls and prepared mugs of steaming coffee. Gulping down her breakfast she hardly dared look at him, still not certain whether what had happened last night had been real, or merely a dream. And whatever he had been going to say to her couldn't have been very important otherwise he'd have spoken by now.

'Let's load up now,' she said when they had finished eating, and five minutes later they drove into the woodland, binoculars and cameras at the ready. The matriarchs and their families were already on their way to the lagoon for their wallow in the mud, swishing the flies away with their trunks.

'I'm hoping we'll spot the two pregnant cows this morning,' Lisa said, turning to Guy and smiling at the thrill of recording this wonder of nature for the film. 'I'm almost certain they're both at full term, though it would be a miracle if the family allowed us to get close enough to see the births clearly.'

In total harmony they worked through

the heat of the morning, hardly stopping except to gulp a few mouthfuls of water and pour some over their heads and down the necks of their shirts.

For Lisa this work was part of a mission that had started one night long ago when Guy had held her hand, while with the other he had stroked the little ivory carving . . .

Suddenly Lisa heard a commotion in the fringe of trees beyond the dambo. Grabbing her binoculars she swung round and focused on the cloud of red dust wafting into the still air. With a gasp she recognised one of the two expectant mothers, pacing up and down — clearly in distress.

Bursting with excitement she signalled to Guy, beckoning him to come quickly.

Guy gestured towards the Land Rover.

She held up her hand, vigorously shook her head and beckoned again.

Slowly and carefully they crept as close as they could. Making sure they remained out of sight, they selected a position overlooking the slight hollow the elephants had chosen for the important event. Guy knelt down and focused on the group. Lisa crouched down next to him, hardly breathing, her Leica steady in her hand.

Then with telephoto lenses fitted and cameras poised, they settled down to wait.

The matriarch stood guard. Around her were the aunts and sisters, and five or six younger females. 'This will be part of their training,' Lisa whispered. 'From an early age they're taught to look after babies. Then when they have their own they'll know how to keep them alive.'

In contrast to the earlier commotion there was a sudden stillness. Even the birds seemed to hold their breath as their constant chatter ceased. Guy glanced at Lisa and smiled to see the rapture on her face.

The cow gave a final bellow and a groan that silenced the entire forest.

She shuddered, shot her trunk into the air, then lowered it as she shuffled round to inspect her tiny offspring.

The baby tried to stand up. Its legs wobbled and it fell down. Again and again it tried, standing and falling, standing and falling, and only now did the aunts and sisters rush in to steady it with the ends of their trunks.

And then the celebrations started. Trumpeting and bellowing and running around in circles. From afar the bulls rumbled. The females fussed over the new arrival, each one behaving as though the baby were her own, and for a while Lisa could see nothing but dust.

Suddenly, as though someone had blown a whistle, the commotion stopped. A minute or two later the dust settled.

'Look, Guy!' Lisa whispered. 'She's curling her trunk around her baby . . . '

Guy lowered his camera, took his handkerchief from his pocket and with the gentlest of touches wiped the tears from Lisa's cheeks.

8

A sudden gust of wind fanned Lisa's face, then just as quickly died away. That's strange, she thought, looking up from the notebook she'd been scribbling in ever since witnessing the birth of the baby elephant.

A fish eagle swooped gracefully across the dambo, leaving its lonely lament suspended in the still air. The only other sound came from the elephants as they tore branches from the trees, throwing up their trunks and closing their eyes in ecstasy as they ate. For the family with the new addition, life had quickly returned to its normal pattern.

But there was that breeze again. Lisa put down her notebook. This time she noticed a narrow bank of dark grey cloud hugging the horizon, its jagged edge reaching skywards like a row of crocodile's teeth. As she watched, it began to unfurl, and within a few minutes was racing up the sky like a fast-forwarded film.

Locked in the tunnel-world bordered by the lens of his camera, Guy seemed unperturbed by the change. Lisa smiled at his intense concentration. As he crouched down she could see the soft curve of his neck where it met the downy wave of his hair . . .

As though sensing her scrutiny, he stood up, a look of disquietude in his eyes. 'The light's changed dramatically,' he said. 'Looks as though we could have an early thunderstorm.'

Lisa gazed across the dry, parched ground. Angry clouds were multiplying by the second and the breeze had freshened. She shook her head.

'It's too early for the rains. It'll blow over soon. Last year it often clouded over in October but nothing really happened until well into November.'

But Guy was no longer looking at the sky. He was standing looking at her with that strange look of hesitancy she frequently noticed on his face. A narrowing of his eyes and a puckering of his brow, as though he was in some kind of dilemma, though she had no idea what this could be.

She glanced at her watch. 'The pontoon will be ready for operation in just over an hour. We should think of going soon.'

Guy said nothing, nor did he make any move to prepare for their departure. He just went on standing there, looking at her.

It would be a relief to get back to Hippo Camp, she thought, turning away. Guy was not himself and she had no idea how to cope with this strange behaviour.

'This is my last film,' she said, peering through her view-finder. 'You may have to rely on my drawings when you're editing this afternoon's footage.'

'We could always come back,' he said, still watching her intently. 'You could photograph any animals you miss today.'

She clutched at her throat. 'In the helicopter next time, I hope. Then we could bring Tony and Iliana — '

'Why, Lisa? Don't you like being alone with me?'

'It makes no difference, one way or the other,' she said, making a valiant attempt at flippancy as she snapped a telephoto lens onto her camera.

Getting no response, she marched away from him and aimed wildly at a young calf with only one tusk. She knew she was wasting her precious dwindling supply of film, but that was better than carrying on this tension-laden conversation.

A moment later Guy was behind her again, so close now that she could feel the warmth of his breath on the back of her head.

'I've been thinking about your views on the factors affecting the elephant populations,' he said, as if the previous conversation had never taken place. 'Which particular aspect should we emphasise in the film, do you think?'

She kept her eyes on the one-tusk elephant. 'I told you, Guy. It's a combination of many things. Habitat restriction — '

'Yes, but we should go more for the psychological repercussions, don't you think? The disruption to the family system due to poaching — that you're always so upset about,' he added slowly.

Ducking in front of her he stood directly between her camera and the one-tusk elephant. 'You told me that if you deprive a calf of its mother it won't grow up with any of the known codes of behaviour. And this could have a knock-on effect — '

His face was almost touching hers now. She could see the fire in his eyes. The same fire she'd seen when she'd been that susceptible teenager without a mother to teach her the accepted codes of behaviour . . .

Dodging sideways she aimed once more at the one-tusk elephant. A fresh blast of wind blew a strand of hair across her eyes. She scraped it behind her ear but it fluttered back again. Disregarding the darkening sky she stumbled towards the calves she'd been photographing earlier and took three more close-ups in quick succession. When the camera suddenly started rewinding she muttered under her breath but kept on moving forward, pretending to take more shots, tears stinging her eyes.

Guy lunged towards her, gripped her arm and pulled her back towards the Land Rover. He wrenched open the door and heaved her on to the seat as though she was a sack of ground maize, then jumped in next to her and grasped both her arms.

'That was a foolish thing to do, Lisa! Didn't you see that they were becoming agitated?'

'Why? What does it matter to you what I do?' She looked down at her hands, still clasping the camera as though not trusting them to be free, then upwards to where Guy's fingers dug into her flesh.

Their eyes were level now. 'Everything you do matters to me, Lisa,' he said in his slow and deliberate way. 'You should know that by now.'

She twisted her head away. 'You're only concerned because you need me for this film!' She closed her eyes tightly, hating herself for her sharp tongue. She had lost her sense of proportion but hadn't been able to stop herself.

She opened her eyes. Was needing people such a crime, she suddenly thought. After all, everyone needed someone else for one reason or another.

Her gaze met his and she swallowed hard before she could bring herself to speak. 'I'm sorry, Guy. I didn't mean that. But you seem to forget I spent all last year working among these elephants — '

'I know, Lisa. But that doesn't give you any special protection over other human beings, does it? Oh, Lisa . . . ' With a deep sigh he let go of her and dropped his head into his hands.

She saw the muscles tighten between his neck and his shoulders. There was something wrong and she wished she knew what it was. 'Guy?' she said softly. 'Guy? What are you trying to say?'

Finally he lifted his head and Lisa had a glimpse of the torment raging inside him. What could be troubling him so much that it had the power to change his normal behaviour to this extent? A successful film-maker. A man at the pinnacle of his career.

'Nothing,' he said, his eyes meeting hers. 'Nothing at all. But I wish you wouldn't do things like that. If anything happened . . . '

His voice drifted off but Lisa had the feeling that the unspoken words were still there inside him. Abruptly he switched his gaze to the gathering clouds. 'The light's too bad to carry on,' he said. 'And in spite of what you say I think we're in for one hell of a storm.'

As he spoke, the first rumble of thunder rolled across the bush. 'Come

159

on. We'd better head for the pontoon before it starts pelting down.'

Ten minutes later two saucer sized drops of rain plopped on to the dusty windscreen. Within another five minutes they could not see more than a yard or two in front of them. Jagged forks of lightening streaked across the blue-black sky, followed almost immediately by crashing thunder that reverberated into the distance.

'I can't see a thing!' Guy yelled, hunching his shoulders as he peered at the wall of water bombarding the windscreen. The Land Rover was slithering from one side of the narrow track to the other and Lisa had to hold on to the dashboard with both hands to stop being hurled out of her seat.

'We can carry on if you like,' he said, shouting to make himself heard above the deafening roar of the rain. 'But I think we should stop and sit it out.'

'No! Let's carry on,' Lisa shouted back, although they were almost at a standstill. 'We must get to the pontoon before six. They don't make any crossings after dark. Not even for a hefty bribe.'

Suddenly the rear wheels began to spin. Guy eased back on the accelerator and changed down into four-wheel drive. A few moments later the engine cut out. Quickly he turned the ignition key. The engine roared into life. He revved but it was no use. The wheels spun and the Land Rover did not move a single inch forward.

Guy leapt out into the surrounding quagmire, undid the shovel from the roof rack and began digging the mud away from the wheels. After five minutes he jumped back into the driver's seat, his clothes drenched, his hair plastered to his head, his face, arms and legs spattered with mud.

'It's impossible,' he gasped, pulling off his muddy boots. 'Until some of the surface water has drained away I'll never dig us out of that lot.'

Lisa watched him peel the sodden

shirt from his body like shedding a second skin. He squeezed it out then hung it on a hook on the side panel. He wiped the mud off his face and gave her a wan smile, then hauled the food hamper onto the front seat.

'Well, it's hardly a feast,' he said, 'but we still have plenty of drinking water and there're a few bananas and oranges left. Help yourself when you're hungry.'

Lisa looked forlornly at the fogged-up windows that imprisoned her. The rain showed no signs of letting up, so after five minutes she dug into her rucksack for her notebook. 'Could we have the light on, please Guy?' she asked, after searching in vain for the switch.

'Yeah, sure. That is, if you want the battery completely flattened.'

Lisa sighed. Now what? She wasn't hungry, but to pass the time she ate a banana, opening the window a fraction to throw away the skin. She sat staring straight ahead. She felt her skin burning as her awareness of Guy intensified with each silent minute, and sensed without looking at him that it was the same for him.

About ten minutes later, as though someone had closed a tap, the deafening deluge stopped. Guy opened the door and shone his torch on the sea of dark mud around them.

'We seem to have sunk in even deeper,' he said. 'We might as well get a good night's sleep. I'll dig us out at daybreak.'

Without a word Lisa opened the passenger door and gingerly stepped down into the squelching mud.

'Don't go far,' Guy said, and handed her the torch.

Holding on to the bedraggled saplings on the edge of the track, she managed to slither a few steps. The smell of dampened dust that comes with the first rain of the season hung in the air. She stopped to take a few deep breaths, storing the evocative smell in her secret shelf of memories that one day in the future would remind her of this night.

When she got back, Guy had rearranged their filming equipment, piling it into one corner of the Land Rover. In the small remaining space he had spread the futon and hung up the net.

She put it off for as long as she could, but finally the mosquitoes won. She took off her muddy boots and climbed into the back.

Guy crawled in next to her and tucked in the net. She rolled over and curled her knees up in front of her. After a few minutes her teeth were still clenched and her nails were digging deep holes into her palms.

With her eyes as wide as a chameleon's she watched the storm move steadily westwards. The rumble of thunder grew more distant and occasional flashes of lightning lit up the sky like a giant fireworks display, outlining the heavy black clouds still drifting across the stars. A sight so mesmerising that she was totally unprepared for the sudden split of lightning that lit up the bush around them like a blaze of searchlights in an old war movie. A simultaneous burst of thunder shook the Land Rover as though a bomb had exploded directly beneath it.

'It's all right, Lisa,' Guy said, folding his arms around her as if she were a little girl. 'It's only thunder.'

'I'm sorry,' she said, mortified that she had not been able to stop her arms and legs shooting out and striking Guy as he lay motionless beside her. 'But there was no warning.'

'I know,' he murmured gently. 'That one was pretty close. We're lucky we weren't hit.'

For a few moments she lay absolutely still. Realising that her head was still resting against Guy's bare chest, she put her hand up to push herself away, but he continued to hold her firmly.

She laughed nervously. He was only doing what he would have done to comfort anyone in distress, she assured herself.

'Guy, I'm okay now. It's daft, I know,

but it's only sudden noises in the dark that do that to me.'

'Don't worry. It's a common enough reaction. I think that was the storm's finale, but if it starts up again, I'll be right here.'

I'll be right here . . .

How reassuring those words were, she thought, gradually relaxing her muscles as the tension ebbed away.

'You're a strange mixture, Lisa. Such a level-headed person. It comes as a bit of a surprise that you should have this fear.'

'I know. It's ridiculous, but — ' She screwed up her eyes as she tried to ward off the memory his words had triggered. But it was all there in front of her now. The darkness, the fear, the pain that wouldn't go away, even after all these years . . .

'But what?' He gave her arm a gentle squeeze, as though to urge her to carry on.

'Well, one night when I was very young . . . ' She paused. 'I'm sure you don't really want to hear this — '

'Go on, Lisa. Tell me. Please.'

'Okay,' she said, and took a few deep breaths. 'I was in bed. My mother and father were arguing. Far worse than usual. I couldn't sleep. I hated them arguing. I wanted them to love each other and to love me. I'm sorry. You probably won't understand this — '

'Oh, but I do, Lisa. I understand very well.'

'I called out to my mother. She didn't hear me. We lived in a big house. Suddenly there was an ear-splitting clap of thunder. The lights went out. I screamed for my mother. She didn't come. I couldn't see to get out of bed. I heard my father yelling, saying the most dreadful things to my mother, and her, screeching back at him. The next minute the front door banged — '

'And then?' Guy asked.

'Nothing. Just silence. The kind of silence that fills the space around you with noises from within yourself.

Humming and buzzing. Booming. Banging. Making you want to scream — '

'And did you scream?' he whispered.

'I screamed but no-one came. I lay in the dark, screaming until I couldn't scream any more. The next day my father came back, but . . . '

'What?'

'He told me my mother was in hospital. I never saw her again.'

'Oh, Lisa.' He propped himself up on his elbow. 'Why didn't you tell me all this before? I knew your mother had died when you were very young and that you'd gone to boarding school, but I'd no idea it was as bad as that.'

'I've never told anyone before,' she said, feeling as though pieces of her had been ripped from her body. 'And I hope I never will again.'

'Telling me, instead of bottling it up inside you, was the best thing you could have done. It's my bet you won't ever be afraid of thunder again.'

She turned to face him. 'I hope you're

right,' she said, managing a sheepish smile.

'I'm sure I am. And do you know why?'

'No. Why?'

'I also had a frightening experience in my childhood. It haunted me for many years — until I told someone about it.'

Lisa couldn't imagine anything happening to Guy that would frighten him. 'What was it?'

'I had three older brothers — '

'Lucky you.'

'Well, yes, it had its advantages. I was the baby, so my parents spoiled me. And that was the trouble really. I got things my brothers didn't get — '

He paused and Lisa had the feeling he had changed his mind and wasn't going to tell her any more. 'And then?' she said.

'One day, when my parents were out and my brothers were looking after me, they decided to teach me a lesson — for accepting those extra luxuries. We had an ancient trunk in the attic — the kind people used to take on long sea voyages. Somehow they inveigled me into this trunk, promising some kind of reward. Then they banged down the lid and ran downstairs. Their laughter got fainter and fainter until I couldn't hear them any more.'

'You mean — they left you there!'

'For hours and hours.'

'You must have been frantic.'

'I shouted myself hoarse. It was pitch dark. I banged on the lid of the trunk until I could feel the stickiness and smell the blood on my knuckles. Then I just lay there, all hunched up, getting colder and colder and more and more terrified. I think they probably forgot all about me until just before my parents got back, because when they got me out they made me promise not to tell anyone — '

'And I suppose you were too afraid to tell on them,' she said. 'I remember that happening to me at boarding school.'

He nodded. 'I never told my parents. Though years later I told one of my teachers at school. Goodness knows why. She just seemed so sympathetic one day when I refused to take my turn to tidy the little dark storeroom that had no windows and no ventilation. I was never scared of a small dark place again.'

'It's no wonder you love nature's wide open spaces.'

Lisa lay absolutely still, trying to picture the panic-stricken boy, trembling in the dark of the trunk, his tiny hands raw and bleeding.

'Guy . . . '

'Hmm?'

'Goodnight, and . . . thanks . . . for telling me. And for listening.' She moved to her side of the futon, wishing she could have sounded more grateful.

Soon she heard the sound of regular breathing. She longed to do the same, but just as she'd done the night before, she lay tense, aware of his nearness and of how ironic it was that she was here with him, so close, yet with so much that kept them distant. That would always keep them distant.

Above the noises of night she heard the swollen river. Twenty yards away? Fifty? It was hard to tell how far they were from its twisting ox-bow banks that every year the raging tide of tropical rains demolished and rearranged. But she knew by the rushing, swishing sounds that the water was in a state of turmoil. So utterly different from the calm waters of the River Isis, where one day when she was only eighteen he had shown her how to photograph extreme light and shade . . .

She closed her eyes. She was waiting for him outside her college residence, sitting on the bench under the oak trees in order to see him the moment he appeared around the side of the ancient creeper-covered building. She looked down at her brightly coloured clothes, wondering if they were appropriate for a day on the river. She was used to wearing pale pastel colours, having given all that horrid navy blue to Oxfam, the day after she left school. 'Wear something red,' he had said, so she'd bought this brilliant red T-shirt. Now she wasn't so sure.

At dead on nine o'clock he appeared, moving towards her with a long, loose stride. He stopped in front of her, smiling.

'You look good enough to eat,' he said.

She blinked as she looked down at her red T-shirt. She wasn't used to men saying things like that to her.

He slung her camera bag over his shoulder. He had an old worn rucksack on his back. 'I've brought a little picnic,' he said as they set off for the river. 'Egg sandwiches. Apples. A flask of coffee.'

At the kiosk on the wooden landing stage where the punts were hired, she stood in the shade of massive old oak trees, while Guy paid the boatman. The sylvan scene took her breath away. It was exactly like the Constable painting her father had in his library at home, with the same aura of tranquillity and timelessness.

The boat was long and narrow, with a flat bottom and square ends. Guy got in first, then helped her in. The boat wobbled. She stumbled. He caught her in his arms. 'You'll soon get used to the movement,' he said as he manoeuvred them away from the bank. The boat made little rippling noises as they glided from sun-sparkled water to the deep shadows cast by overhanging willow trees lining the banks.

'Don't be afraid to point the camera at the sun,' he said. 'Throw away convention. Be original. Let it be shocking, even ugly, but let it be the truth . . . '

He tied up to an old rusty ring on the bank. He sat down opposite her. His hands moved towards her, slowly, almost as though they were not moving at all, until she didn't know where to look. His eyes were drawn together, as so often they were, as though in pain. He shook his head, squeezed his eyes tightly shut, then with a sigh he took the camera from her hands . . .

Lisa opened her eyes and realised she must have been asleep. Shadows became shapes. Blacks became greys. Numbness became tingling. And then the rumblings of the elephants reached her ears and she knew where she was.

Guy had turned over onto his back and was murmuring something incomprehensible. To move suddenly would surely waken him. Perhaps she could just shrink away from him, without actually moving . . .

For a few minutes she lay absolutely still. It was the most comforting, secure feeling she'd ever had, but it was getting lighter and the birds had begun their morning songs in earnest. She would have to hurry before he woke up and discovered them like this.

Quickly, before she could change her mind, she moved away. She glanced at Guy's face. He was still asleep. A stubble of blond beard covered his chin. His mouth curved softly in repose with no hint of the unease that these days so often clouded his expression.

Sliding silently out of the net, she slipped into her mud-encrusted boots and stepped down, surprised to find solid mud instead of the squelching, liquid morass of last night.

She unscrewed the top of the water bottle and had a drink, then used a little to have a quick wash before going for a stroll in the bush in the faint hope of finding some dry kindling.

When she returned, Guy was crouching down next to the Land Rover, his elbows wedged against his chest, one eye looking through the viewfinder of his camera.

'Just keep walking,' he said. 'Don't look at me. Don't smile. Just keep looking exactly the way you look now . . . '

9

Approaching Hippo Camp, Lisa could see Tony and Iliana waiting to greet them. Enoch and Joseph and the rest of the camp helpers were lined up next to them, all waving and smiling. When the dust settled, Tony thrust a small bundle of letters above his head, waggling them to attract Guy's attention.

'Are we glad to see you,' Tony said. 'That was some storm.'

As Guy started unpacking his cameras and equipment, Iliana strolled over to the Land Rover and peered into the back. The rolled up futon and mosquito net were clearly visible.

She stabbed the ground with the heel of her boot. 'I have never spent the night in the back of a Land Rover. Was it comfortable, Lisa?'

'It was . . . okay,' Lisa said, keeping her eyes lowered.

'Don't you want to see the mail?' Tony said, handing the letters to Guy. 'Had a radio message last night from the post office about a special delivery to the Kilanga rest camp. Picked them up first thing this morning. All three have London postmarks,' he added. 'Two from Eagle Films London office. And one personal — for you, Guy. All marked urgent.'

Guy tore open the first thick envelope with the Eagle Films logo on the front. Quickly he scanned the pages. 'The rushes report!' he said with a deep intake of breath. 'Everything's spot-on, thank goodness! Now we can really forge ahead.'

When he read the second letter from Eagle he let out a long, slow sigh, but made no comment.

Tony stood watching Guy stuff the letters into his pocket and carry on unpacking.

'Guy?' he said, a look of incredulity on his face. 'What about the one in the long cream envelope? It sure looks important.'

'Just a routine report, I expect,' Guy said without looking at Tony. 'I'll read it later.'

'But it's marked urgent.'

With an impatient shrug he whipped the remaining envelope from his pocket. He opened it and unfolded the single sheet of paper. With a sudden gasp he closed his eyes, then opened them and reread the letter as though he hadn't believed the contents the first time.

Lisa saw his face drain to a greyish white.

Finally he put it in his pocket. He looked about to speak, but after a moment of stillness he turned and strode to his tent, his head slumped down into his shoulders.

★ ★ ★

Peering through the slits in the slatted bamboo walls of the roofless shower cubicle, Lisa sensed an uncomfortable silence around the camp. All she could hear was the constant screech of cicadas and the occasional grunt of a hippo or a splash as an elephant flopped into the river. Letting the water cascade over her body from the bucket suspended above her head, she wondered what devastating news the long cream envelope had contained.

Left on her own she spent the rest of the day working in her tent, making sure she had accurate descriptions of each elephant Guy had filmed over the past two days. Finally she looked up from her laptop, admitting to herself that professionally it was thrilling to find their work dovetailing so rewardingly.

She was packing everything away when she heard Joseph's drums throb through the camp announcing that in fifteen minutes dinner would be ready.

She had just pulled on her jeans when she heard a low murmur of voices coming from Guy's tent. She strained to catch the words, but the evening chatter of Carmine Bee-eaters nesting on the banks of the river made it impossible to hear everything clearly.

'But Guy, you said you liked it?' There was a sob in Iliana's voice.

'It's too soon, Iliana ... I can't promise ... '

Lisa kept absolutely still, afraid of alerting the speakers to her eavesdropping.

'I can not bear it ... this waiting ... ' Iliana went on, her Spanish accent more marked than ever.

'One day, Iliana, if we are patient ... '

Lisa clamped her hands over her ears. Thank *goodness* the filming would be completed in a few weeks and she need *never* see him again.

* * *

When she'd finished dressing, Lisa strolled past the river towards the fig tree, a pang of regret pulling at the muscles in her chest. Yesterday she had begun to think she had misjudged Guy, but it was clear to her now that he hadn't changed a bit. He was as much like her father as he ever was. Breathing in the sultry air of the approaching dusk she forced herself to forget what she had heard. It was none of her business, so let him get on with it. She would erase the past. She would carry on working with Guy as long as he needed her and then she would never see him again.

Fascinated by the reflected flashes of orange and indigo dancing on the water like the ever-changing shapes in a kaleidoscope, she didn't see Guy until she heard his voice — right beside her.

'Sit here, Lisa,' he said, pulling out the chair next to his.

Fifty yards upstream a line of elephants moved in silhouette across the bejewelled surface of the river. Guy followed Lisa's gaze.

'It's incredible,' he said, 'but through you I feel I really understand them now. They're intelligent. With strong emotions — ' He paused, and looked at her.

'Just like you and me . . . '

With his words still dangling in mid-air Guy took a bottle of white wine from the ice bucket on the table. He handed her a glass and folded his fingers over hers. She had the feeling that he was about to tell her something but at that moment Iliana and Tony arrived at the table. Still looking at Lisa, Guy stood up and pulled out a chair for Iliana, then poured two more glasses of wine.

Tony looked askance at Guy, clearly wondering what had prompted the opening of a bottle of wine, a rare treat in the bush.

When Guy remained silent Tony raised his glass.

'Well, let's drink to the rushes report then, shall we,' he said, curling his arm possessively around a despondent looking Iliana.

But as hard as Tony tried to liven things up, it was Guy's pensive mood that set the tone for the entire evening. As soon as the meal was over Lisa decided to escape to her tent and read her book.

As she stood up Guy's arm shot out to stop her.

'Don't go yet, Lisa. There's something you have to know. There's something you all have to know. Sit down, please.'

Lisa watched his face and saw the lines of torment around his eyes, saw his mouth quiver at the corners. As she waited for him to speak it was as if something was about to happen that would change her life forever.

'I think I'd better start at the beginning,' Guy said. But instead of speaking he clamped his hands to the sides of his head and like a man demented he began pacing up and down. First around the table and then away from the table towards the grassy fringe just beyond the open space surrounding the fig tree. Lisa had never before seen him display so much anguish, though come to think of it she realised now that she'd seen this building up ever since they'd arrived back in Hippo Camp.

Was it something to do with Iliana, she wondered? Or with the film? Or was it the letter in the long cream envelope? Something catastrophic that he needed to share with them but found too difficult to say?

Suddenly he jumped backwards. But it was too late. The short thick snake had reared up and buried its fangs into Guy's leg.

'It's a puff adder!' Lisa yelled, leaping up and recognising with a sick feeling the brownish black diamond pattern of Africa's most deadly snake. If she didn't act quickly nothing could be done to save him.

'Make him lie down!' she screeched to Tony and Iliana. 'Hold him down! Don't let him walk! Drag him away from the grass but don't let him move whatever you do! I'll get my kit!'

Running faster than she'd ever done in her life she was back at Guy's side in less than a minute with the square tin open, still cold from the fridge, and the syringe loaded with the serum. She slid the needle into his calf muscle just above the two tiny black holes, then slowly pushed the plunger into the barrel of the syringe, her heart thudding against her ribs.

She stayed kneeling at his side, watching his face, numbed by what had happened. 'For once it's a good thing you aren't wearing your boots,' she said shakily. 'Otherwise he'd have struck higher up — nearer your heart.'

Guy looked at her aghast as she held his wrist to take his pulse. She saw no pain in his eyes, only an intensification of the look of agitation she'd seen earlier.

'Tony, get on the radio quickly,' she said. 'Tell them to send the helicopter. Then ask the clinic to stand by and call the doctor in — if there is one. Guy, don't move! I'm tempted to apply a tourniquet, but this can sometimes do more harm than good. We can't take a chance — '

'You could put it round my neck,' Guy said with a half-hearted grin, but Lisa knew his attempt to crack a joke was merely to mask his fear.

She cradled his head in her hands. 'Guy, don't talk and don't move,' she said as she waited for Tony to make contact with the airstrip.

'What?' Tony screamed into the radio. 'Still no fuel?'

'Okay Tony, get the Cruiser!' Lisa shouted. 'Bring it in as close as you can. Joseph and Enoch will carry you, Guy. Any movement will increase your circulation. We *must* stop the poison from reaching your heart. We have one hour at the most — *if* you keep still. So let's go. How long to the clinic, Tony?'

'Fifty minutes — if there are no streams in flood,' Tony said. 'And if we're lucky,' he muttered to himself in between screaming into the radio telling the staff at the clinic it was a matter of life and death and they had to have a doctor come hell or high water.

'Now,' Tony said to the clinic. 'Yes,

we're leaving now . . . No, in a four-by-four. We can't get the aircraft . . . Yes, we've injected the serum . . . No, I don't know if the serum is still active.'

As Tony swung the Cruiser away from the camp, Lisa saw Joseph and Enoch standing in a huddle with the rest of the camp staff, the sticks they had used to beat the snake to death still in their hands, their faces, lit by the sweep of the headlights, filled with terror.

The journey was a nightmare. 'I never realised before just how bumpy this track was,' Tony said, trying to drive as fast as possible but at the same time keep Guy still enough for the poison not to travel towards his heart.

Lisa held Guy's shoulders down as he lay on the back seat, his head in her lap. 'I just hope they've got a doctor,' she said, remembering the team member last year whose broken leg was set by a student nurse. 'Sometimes they do. Sometimes they don't. The doctors never stay long.'

Shining the torch on to Guy's grey face she felt a burning sensation inside her. A sensation she couldn't put a name to but which made her feel as though every bone, every tendon, every muscle was about to snap in two. Pain? Yes, pain, but pain because of what? Fear, pity, regret? Love? Could this feeling be love after all?

As she stared at him he opened his eyes and she had the feeling that in those few moments before he closed them again he had known exactly what her thoughts were.

'Don't move, Guy. Keep your eyes closed. The poison reaches the heart through the slightest exertion . . . '

Suddenly she remembered the frantic radio conversation between Tony and the clinic, just before they'd left Hippo Camp. The serum! She hadn't checked the expiry date. There hadn't been time . . .

★ ★ ★

A stretcher was waiting at the entrance, a drip stand beside it. There was no doctor but an efficient looking Sister in a crisp white uniform took over as soon as they arrived and knew what she was doing. Within minutes the drip was up and Guy was in bed and all routine checks completed.

'If he hasn't gone into a coma in another hour, he has a chance,' she whispered in Lisa's ear. 'And in twelve hours — if there's still no sign of coagulation — he should be fine.'

She smiled at Lisa. 'You're sure you gave him the correct serum?'

Lisa felt as though everything in her stomach was about to be ejected. 'Yes,' she whispered, closing her eyes and swallowing hard and mentally crossing her fingers. 'Absolutely sure.'

'I've given him a sedative,' the Sister said. 'He should sleep till morning. Please, will you all wait on the veranda. And try not to worry. The nurse will keep a close watch.'

'No!' Lisa said. '*I'll* watch him. I'll

call you if there's any change.' She remained steadfastly at the foot of the bed, her eyes glued to Guy's closed eyes, everything else in the ward a blur. One hour, the Sister had said, and then another twelve hours. No, she wasn't going anywhere until she knew Guy was safe.

'Please, you will wait on the veranda,' the Sister insisted. But as Iliana and Tony silently trooped out, Lisa stood her ground.

'Very well,' the Sister said, her face softening as she took in the look of agony on Lisa's face. 'Here's the bell. Press it at once if you see the slightest change. Breathing, colour, movement — anything. I'll be back shortly to check his pulse and temperature.'

As soon as the Sister had left the room Lisa tiptoed to the side of the bed. She knelt down, and holding Guy's limp hand in her own she lowered her head to his chest.

Guy opened his eyes a fraction. He saw that Lisa's cheeks were glistening, like dew on petals in the early morning. He wanted to touch them but his hands refused to move. She was whispering something — just one word — over and over again. He strained to hear what she was saying, and then, through the haze of his sedation, he realised what it was.

'Live! Live! Live!' she was saying, over and over and over again.

Iliana, standing in the shadow of the doorway, turned away.

When the vital hour was finally up and Guy had not gone into a coma, Lisa thought that it was she who'd been given a new lease of life — not Guy. A wave of recognition had swept over her. It had been like walking through a mist. As each second of each minute had passed the mist had become clearer, and now she knew she didn't care any more what he had done in the past. Or what he might do in the future. All she knew was that no matter how far apart they were she would always love him.

'You've recovered remarkably well,' Lisa said a few days later when they were having breakfast under the fig tree, 'but I really think you ought to take it easy — '

'Taking it easy is not an option,' Guy said, leaving his plate half-empty as he marched off to collect the cameras and film he needed for the day's shoot.

'He has not been like this before,' Iliana whispered when Guy was out of earshot. 'He is so quiet. Never has he worked so hard, and yet he looks so sad. I wonder what he was going to tell us just before the snake attacked him.'

'Perhaps he was never meant to tell us,' Lisa said, twisting away from Iliana's probing gaze. 'Perhaps he never will. Perhaps he decided the news in the letter was too painful and too personal to share with anyone else.'

Just lately Lisa often found the girl staring at her when she thought she wasn't looking. In spite of her extrovert

193

personality Iliana was a very private person, and Lisa never knew what she was really thinking. She was looking intently at Lisa now, and Lisa felt that somehow Guy's brush with death had forged a bond between them.

'You should also take it easy, Lisa,' she said at last. 'You have dark circles under your eyes, as though you are not sleeping very well.'

*   *   *

The weeks flew by. Sometimes Lisa wished for them to be over quickly and sometimes she prayed for every second to be stretched to an hour. The snakebite had had a sobering effect on the entire team and on the camp staff. Although they were all working together to meet the deadline, she felt lonely, especially as just lately Tony and Iliana seemed to have drawn closer together. Perhaps because Guy was not only aloof with her, but also with Iliana.

Lisa was often in Guy's company for

up to sixteen hours a day, but always with someone else present. He made no attempt to be alone with her, and with the heat and humidity increasing each day in the build up to the start of the rainy season, soon the strain of being with him, yet not able to talk to him alone, became almost unbearable.

Lisa had stopped counting the days but suddenly they were celebrating the team's last night in Africa. Tony opened their one and only bottle of champagne, kept specially for the final night.

Lisa watched them with a tinge of envy. Tony and Iliana were on a high, looking forward to the post-production work in London, and for once, even Guy seemed to relax.

After dinner — steak and Lisa's favourite *boerewors* — Guy stood up and banged the empty champagne bottle on the table.

Was this to be the momentous announcement at last? Lisa wondered.

'Congratulations,' he said to the team. 'You've all done a magnificent job and I thank you.' He swept his arm around to include each and every one of the helpers, who had gathered round to listen to Guy's speech.

At the end of his speech he turned to Lisa. 'I owe you more than you'll ever know,' he said, looking straight into her eyes. 'Although you've chosen to stay on to complete your project for KEA, you'll be with us in spirit. Without you we wouldn't be where we are now. Without you, *I* would certainly not be here,' he added with a faint smile.

Lisa bit her lip. This was his first reference to her saving his life. There was so much she wanted to say, but the lump in her throat prevented her from speaking. She knew she should be as elated as the rest of the team, but nothing she did lifted the feeling of depression she felt descending on her.

Hours later, when the party had long since broken up and the generator had stopped, she was still awake. Struggling out of the net she felt for her torch and unzipped her tent flap. Disoriented by the weeks of intensive work and very little sleep, she staggered into the cool night air. Following the dazzling sweep of the Milky Way, her eyes came to rest on the Southern Cross, the magnificent constellation dominating the southern sky.

Then something caught her eye — a flicker of light in the darkness ahead. Must be the glinting eyes of a small animal, she thought, and began stepping carefully towards the river. Perhaps if she sat out here for a while, the fresh air would make her sleepy.

The moon had just appeared above the trees, throwing its liquid silver across the water, when she saw the silhouette of someone sitting on the old ebony log, close to the river.

'I hoped it might be you when I heard footsteps,' Guy said, flashing his torch as he came towards her. 'What on earth are you doing out here, Lisa?'

Goose pimples spread from her toes to her fingertips.

'Why, you're frozen,' he said as he propelled her to the log. 'I hope you're not getting malaria. Have you been taking your pills?'

'You're always asking me that. There's nothing wrong. I couldn't sleep, that's all.'

Lisa felt the flutter of his breath on her cheek. Why was she always so helpless when he was close to her? What was it about him that always stripped away her common sense and robbed her of her faculties of reasoning? He may have felt gratitude for her prompt action in saving his life, but his recent aloofness was proof that that was where it ended. She should pull away now, before this warm feeling was fired into flame.

'Did you come out here looking for me?' he asked.

'No. I . . . I just wanted some air. I must go back — '

'Don't go,' he said, holding her gently. 'You look so lovely in the moonlight . . . '

Words, words, thought Lisa. 'I didn't mean to disturb you, Guy. I must get some sleep.'

Suddenly he let go of her. 'You know,' he said. 'You and I make a pretty good team. You could join Eagle Films — on a permanent basis, I mean.' He cocked his head and smiled. 'Well? How about it?'

She felt a sinking feeling in her chest. Work. Films. That was all he thought about these days.

'I've got months of work ahead of me here, Guy. Possibly years. If I choose to.'

'Wait till you've seen the finished product and realise it's something you've helped to create. Seeing your work on screen spurs you on to do more. My next film will spotlight the tragedy of the baby turtles at Heron Island on the Great Barrier Reef. You'll love it there.'

Following him around the world, no matter how satisfying her contribution to Eagle Films might be, or how exotic the location, would be sheer folly. Watching Iliana — or some other woman — drooling over him, and having to work in close contact with him the way she had these past few weeks, would be intolerable. No matter how she felt.

'I'm very busy. I don't know when I'll even get the chance to see the film. I'm afraid the answer's no,' she said, feeling as though a bubble in her chest was about to explode. 'Besides, as you well know, my speciality is elephants.'

Only once before had she known a feeling as intense as this. She closed her eyes tightly and in her mind's eye she saw them holding the little ivory elephant between them. She even heard the music that had been playing at the time, could feel it throbbing through her body . . .

For a moment she wavered. If she walked away right now maybe the feeling would go away. But although his body was absolutely still it seemed to radiate a kind of cosmic power, as if its strength came from a source of energy unknown on this planet; energy against which no normal human being could fight.

His arms were rigid at his sides as though someone had tied a rope around them. His skin had a bluish tint in the moonlight. Suddenly he blinked his eyes and opened his mouth. She felt his hands move to her arms and wondered what would happen next — just as she had on that night five years ago, when she'd been certain that at last he was going to tell her he loved her . . .

But this time Lisa had no illusions. This time she knew there was no future. This time she knew he would tire of her again. Oh, if only she could be the one to make him change, but that would be impossible. Men like her father and Guy Barrington never changed.

She would love him from afar. Nobody could stop her doing that. She had already resigned herself to having to face life without the one person in the whole world she was capable of loving. Because she knew now, without any doubt whatsoever, that she could not fight it any longer.

'I didn't think you could grow more beautiful,' Guy said, oblivious of the turmoil inside her. 'But you have.' Gently he turned her into the light of the moon. His mouth was close to hers. Again Lisa wavered, but the spell was broken. The fine strand that had momentarily held them together had snapped. With each second that ticked by she felt the gap widening.

And this time, she told herself, it would be forever.

Pulling away from him she picked up her torch. 'I must go,' she said and began walking to her tent.

Inside she felt a searing pain as if she was losing something that would never again come within her reach. Yet she could not help it. Some other being that was not herself was guiding her movements, forcing her to take actions that were not her own and putting words into her mouth.

She'd been a fool and this must be her conscience leading her down the only sensible path there was. Away from what was never meant to be.

Tossing and turning on her narrow camp bed she tried to imagine what tomorrow would be like. By tomorrow night he would be gone. Five thousand miles would separate them but it might as well be five million.

With the kind of numb sensation that only comes with total finality, she buried her head in the pillow.

10

Lisa had been dreading the journey to Lusaka. She could have kicked herself for agreeing to get a lift in the helicopter. How much better to have said goodbye at Hippo Camp, instead of this long drawn-out parting that would only end at ten-thirty tonight at the International Airport. But it had seemed churlish to argue. 'We can pick up your Land Rover from the garage in Lusaka,' Guy had suggested. 'I can test drive it to make sure everything's in order. After we've left, you can check in at the Pamodzi, have a good night's sleep, see the Director of Wildlife in the morning, then drive back to your camp at your leisure.'

The clattering drone of the helicopter was deafening. Out of the corner of her eye she glanced at Guy. He was looking straight ahead, his outline silhouetted against the dawn sky. Not being able to look at him was agonising. But suddenly she didn't care. On the pretext of watching the sunrise she turned to face him.

I won't ever look at him like this again, high above the African bush, the sun splashing the sky with deep orange. I must imprint this on my mind's eye. Every line and contour of his face, so that I'll be able to see him whenever I want to — exactly the way he is now. I won't even have to close my eyes and he'll be there in front of me . . .

Guy turned to intercept her gaze. He bent his head close to hers so that his mouth was almost touching her ear. 'Penny for them?' he said, above the clatter of the engine.

It took her a moment to compose herself. He had been so different these past few weeks. Not that he'd ignored her. Far from it. In their feverish rush to complete the filming he had worked more and more closely with her as each day went by. But not once had he arranged a meeting with just the two of them alone.

'It'll be strange when you've all gone,' she answered, forcing a smile.

'You can get back to your research, uninterrupted. Isn't that what you wanted?'

He was looking at her now as though there was nobody else in the helicopter but the two of them. The way he used to look at her, before he received the letter in the long cream envelope.

'Yes. I've a lot to catch up,' she said wondering desperately how she would get through the rest of the day, when already she found the strain too much to bear.

★   ★   ★

It was even more difficult in the check-in queue at Lusaka Airport. The queue moved unbearably slowly. The heat was intense, the noise ear-shattering. And although they were all trying their best to keep the conversation on a light level, Lisa knew the others couldn't wait to board the plane. Unable to share their excitement at the prospect of completing the film in London, she wished more than ever that she had stayed in the bush.

'This is when the *really* hard work begins,' Guy said. 'We have the footage — the basic material — thanks to you, Lisa. Now it's time to mould the final shape.'

With a sudden stab of envy Lisa wished she could be a part of that creation. Perhaps she'd been a fool to turn down Guy's offer. But in spite of the professional satisfaction — and the immense sense of achievement if the film were to halt the slaughter of the African elephant — there'd be nothing but agony if she agreed.

'And if you change your mind you just have to let us know,' Guy said, uncannily picking up her thoughts.

Lisa smiled and nodded. 'I will,' she murmured, hardly able to speak, knowing that to move out of his orbit was the only way she would have any peace. By the time she got back to London he would have left for Heron Island. She would never see him again. This was how it had to be.

It didn't help either, that each time he looked at her his eyes would draw together and then they would open wider and his lips would part as though he was about to tell her something. Each time he did this her spirits would lift, only to see him lower his head or turn the other way.

Suddenly they were at the head of the queue. Lisa stood aside while the formalities were completed. In a daze she watched him walk away from her, through the Immigration barrier, down the long passage, out of her life, his neck craned round until the very last moment before he vanished.

And she, glued to the concrete floor. Doing everything in her power not to break through the barrier and run after him . . . Like a bizarre scene in a futuristic Time Travel movie where she was frozen in time while he carried on his normal everyday action.

Outside the airport building she followed the flashing lights of the plane until they dissolved into the dark of the sky. Still clutching her sodden handkerchief she got into her Land Rover and drove blindly into the night.

★ ★ ★

For the next six weeks Lisa had no timetable, no clock. When the elephants slept, she slept. And this was not very often, for they only ever took short cat-naps, slowly lowering their enormous bodies to the ground, rolling over and for ten or fifteen minutes looking as though they were dead.

She was seldom hungry and was often satisfied with a slice of pawpaw and some fruit juice. Now and then she threw a mixture of tinned food into a wok and stir-fried a meal that she hardly ever finished. She could feel the weight dropping off her. Her hair grew to her shoulders and her skin glowed with a light golden tan.

But on the inside there was no glow. Only a sense of shock and disbelief that Guy was gone, and that the empty space he had left would never again be filled.

To compensate, she threw herself into her work with renewed energy. Sensing her single-minded determination to complete her research before the rains intensified, Enoch matched her enthusiasm. He had learned quite a few more words of English. Between them they developed a workable language and Lisa was grateful for his innate understanding of the elephants and his compassion for their plight.

At the end of November she booked her return flight to London.

* * *

'You've done a great job,' Monica said, when soon after Lisa's arrival they met for lunch. 'And it's incredible that in spite of the delay, you completed the assignment in record time. We've all decided we'd like you on our permanent staff.'

Lisa couldn't wish for greater praise. KEA was at the forefront of the battle to save the elephant population of Africa. 'I'm greatly honoured, Monica. And I adore elephants. But I think I ought to diversify a bit. I'll probably end up devoting my life to them, but right now I'm taking a break.'

What she did not tell Monica was that right now every time she thought about an elephant she also thought about Guy. If an assignment abroad came up tomorrow she would leap at it, as long as it was not working with elephants. The sooner she got out of London again, the better. Away from any place on earth where she might meet him.

Monica narrowed her eyes. 'That's all very well,' she said. 'But isn't it time you thought about devoting part of your life to . . . you know . . . a family?'

'It's different for you,' Lisa said quickly. 'You met the right man.'

'And I'm tempted to think that you have too.'

There was a question mark in Monica's voice but Lisa had no doubt that as usual her friend had correctly assessed her feelings. There seemed nothing Lisa could say in reply without revealing the hopelessness of the situation.

'And . . . well, to be honest, Lisa, I had hoped that working in Zambia with Guy Barrington might have changed your mind. It is possible, you know, to combine a career with marriage.'

Lisa gave her friend a sharp look. 'If anything, it made me even more certain that marriage is out of the question for me.'

'Well, it's your life, Lisa. I just hope you aren't depriving yourself of possible happiness for the wrong reasons.'

'Monica . . . ' She had been about to remind her friend that it was she who right at the beginning had warned her against Guy. 'Oh, look at the time! I must fly. Thanks for lunch. Do keep in touch.'

'Take care, Lisa,' she said, kissing her on both cheeks.

Two days later Monica rang again. *'Lisa!'*

'You sound excited. What's up?'

'I've just had an invitation to attend a preview of 'The New Dawn'. Come with me. We could have a meal afterwards. Ian's taken the children to Scotland for a few days — '

'Monica. What *are* you talking about? What's 'The New Dawn?''

'Oh, Lisa. It's *your* film! Don't tell me you haven't let Guy know you're back?'

'No. And I don't intend to.'

'Oh. All right. But I think you're crazy. Look, if you change your mind the preview's on Thursday at three, in that studio in Wardour Street where we launched our first TV appeal. Drinks and snacks first — '

'Thanks for thinking of me, Monica, but I just don't have the time. I'm doing a short job for World Wildlife. Flying to Kenya the following day. I'll be packing — '

'So soon! Well, it was just a thought.'

★   ★   ★

As Lisa paid the taxi driver she saw Monica waiting anxiously outside the studio doors.

'I had a feeling you'd weaken,' she said, smiling broadly as they walked up the steps together. 'It would have been criminal to miss the preview. Besides, everybody's here. The press, TV, reps from all the wildlife associations, diplomats from most African countries — a rare chance for you to meet everyone connected with our work.'

'My curiosity got the better of me,' Lisa admitted as they signed their names at a table near the entrance. 'I've a splitting headache but it occurred to me that as I'm leaving tomorrow I'd even miss it on TV, so this was my only chance of seeing it.'

'Are you sure you're okay? You look pale,' Monica said. 'In spite of your fabulous tan.'

'Just a bit tired. I'll be fine.'

'It's a good title, isn't it?' Monica said.

'Guy told me his titles don't come to him till the end of the editing. I wonder why he called it 'The New Dawn'?'

Champagne glasses covered a trestle table in front of the small private bar. Waiters in starched white suits were passing round delicious looking bite-sized snacks when a deep voice behind them made Lisa freeze. She had known she'd be taking a chance, but had counted on him being far too busy with all the VIPs to notice her presence.

A flush of colour drenched her cheeks. 'Hello Guy,' she said.

'Lisa! I can't believe it! I'd have sent you an invitation if I'd known you were back!'

He was dressed in a beautifully cut charcoal grey suit with a pale yellow silk shirt open at the neck. His blond hair glowed in the artificial lighting and there were still traces of his golden tan.

There was a moment of stillness when neither of them spoke. It was as if the clock had turned back — as if he were looking at her for the very first time.

It's no different, Lisa thought, panicking. My reaction to this man is beyond my control. It always has been. He still has the power to churn my insides into a tight knot, but at the same time make my knees feel like jelly. Which is the last thing I want to happen now, surrounded by the critical eyes of the zoological world, with press cameras whirring and clicking all around us.

'You must be pleased you made the deadline,' she managed to say.

'I couldn't have done it without you.'

'You're very kind,' she answered as nonchalantly as she could. 'Where's Iliana?' she asked, the words spilling involuntarily from her lips.

'She e-mailed me from — I think it

was Reykjavik.' He removed a sheaf of printouts from his pocket and handed one to Lisa.

'*Know it will be a winner. See you in two weeks. All my . . .* ' The words swam in front of Lisa's eyes and silently she handed it back to Guy.

'She's writing the music for a new series of ITV commercials,' he said, glancing at his watch. 'She was upset at not getting the contract for 'The New Dawn' but I knew that if she was patient it would happen sooner or later. A lucky break for her and Tony — especially on their honeymoon. Look, Lisa, I must dash now. My BBC interview is about to begin. I'll call you . . . No, how about dinner tonight — if you're free? See you later . . . '

Lisa stared blankly at his back, her mouth slightly open.

'The adrenaline's flowing,' Monica said, her eyes following Guy across the room as she sidled up to Lisa. 'He's enjoying the publicity, and it's no wonder the media can't get enough of him. He's even sexier than he was at Oxford! Who's Iliana?' she asked.

Still trying to assimilate the news about Iliana and Tony, Lisa hesitated. 'Er . . . oh, she's . . . just a sound recordist. Works freelance for Eagle Films. Writes music'

'Then why was it that when you were reading that e-mail from her, your mouth dropped open, and — '

Just then one of the BBC officials took hold of Lisa's hand and led her quickly through the crowd towards the battery of cameras and reporters. 'Sorry about that,' he said, placing her next to Guy in the line-up facing the cameras. 'We would have called you earlier but we hadn't realised you'd be here.'

Afterwards Lisa couldn't remember anything she'd said. She couldn't even remember the questions the interviewers had asked. All she remembered was the way her body had shuddered every time Guy put his arm around her — albeit for the benefit of the cameras.

And later, when the film was finished

and the roar of applause had died down, the warm feeling of pride, of belonging to the team, even banished for a short while the growing weakness she had felt coming on since morning.

She caught Monica looking at her with a puzzled frown. Her headache had been worsening all afternoon but had been kept at bay by the excitement of seeing Guy and then seeing the film. But suddenly she knew that something was wrong. A cold sweat had broken out all over her body as though an icy tap had been turned on.

Faces swam around her. Strong arms grasped her as the ground slid from under her feet.

'My car's right outside,' she heard a deep voice say.

Moments later Monica was propping her up on the back seat of Guy's BMW.

'Thanks, Monica,' the voice said. 'I'll drive her to my flat in St. John's Wood. Here's the number. Stay in touch . . . '

And that was the last thing Lisa heard.

11

Lisa looked down at her unusual apparel as the strange room swam into focus.

'How long have I been here?' she whispered, blinking her eyes.

Guy moved swiftly to the bed and knelt down beside her.

'I thought you'd never ask,' he said.

Lisa wondered what he was doing here. And why his usually deep voice sounded so peculiar, as though his vocal chords had been damaged. Perhaps it's because I'm still dreaming, she thought, narrowing her eyes to try to see him more clearly and remembering how sometimes if a dream was really special she could inveigle herself back into it even after she had woken up. Was this one of those?

She looked down at her blue and white striped arms. 'Where am I? And why am I wearing *this?*'

'Your fever was very high. In two days you've gone through my entire wardrobe of pyjama tops, young lady. The laundry service has been struggling to keep up!'

'You mean . . . ?' She looked around the room, frowning as reality overtook the dream.

'I didn't think you'd want to go into hospital,' he said quickly, smoothing her rumpled sheet. 'A friend who special-ises in tropical medicine did the blood test, gave me the necessary drugs to combat the malaria — and the rest was easy.'

He rested his hand on top of hers. 'Don't you remember . . . anything at all?' He smiled at her, eyebrows raised and lips slightly puckered.

A deluge of possible scenarios tumbled through Lisa's mind. 'No,' she said, draw-ing her hand away. 'Not really . . . ' And then she remembered Kenya. 'Guy! What day is it?'

'Don't panic. Monica cancelled your

flight and phoned World Wildlife.' He looked at her closely then briefly held the back of his hand against her forehead. 'You had me worried for a while, Lisa. Why on earth didn't you take your anti malaria pills?'

'I *did* — ' She put her hand to her mouth. 'At least — I think I did, but my final week was such a rush . . . '

He was leaning over her, his face only inches from hers. She had a sudden urge to kiss him. Maybe it was the malaria drugs she'd been on that were playing havoc with her inhibitions. She'd heard how some of them could cause hallucinations.

She took a long deep breath and forced herself to think clearly. The sooner she got out of here the better. Away from the dreamlike quality of these surroundings that were warping her judgement. She had a job to do and already she was goodness knows how many days late.

'Thank you for everything, Guy,' she said, watching his eyes, seeing in them the empathy, the kindness, the concern and all the other things that had always made her love him — apart from the one thing that could never be overcome. 'I can't use up any more of your time.' She swallowed hard. 'So I'll get up now and move back to my flat — '

'Lisa, what's the rush? What is it about me that makes you so restless?'

She pushed herself up on her elbows, carefully avoiding touching him. 'We have our own paths to follow. We always have had.'

What more was there to say? She didn't want to sound ungrateful but neither did she want to have to say the hateful words, the words she knew would hurt her more to utter than to leave unspoken.

Pushing the bedclothes aside she swung her legs to the side of the bed. Before her feet had even touched the floor, the walls and ceiling of the room began revolving around her. As she fell into Guy's waiting arms, she closed her eyes tightly.

'You're not strong enough to go anywhere,' he said, easing her down and pushing her dishevelled hair off her face. 'Besides, there's a great deal to discuss. When I come back we'll talk.'

Discuss? Talk? What did he mean?

She opened her eyes and thank goodness the room had stopped spinning. Guy was putting on his jacket. 'Where are you going?' she asked.

'Oh, a bit of shopping. And I must organise some food. I won't be long, so don't you dare move until I get back.'

He's different, Lisa thought, as the door closed behind him. Ever since the terrible day when he received the letter in the long cream envelope — the day he was bitten by the snake — he'd been quiet, subdued, thoughtful, quite unlike his usual self. Today he was brighter, more carefree, and yet he still seemed to have something on his mind. Something he wasn't sharing with her.

Gradually she lifted her head from the pillows and looked around the room. A typical male domain, devoid of the frills or foibles normally attributable to the female sex, it had only one untidy corner containing a desk piled high with papers, with a leather chair in front of it. It would be nice to get out of this bed and sit upright for a while, she thought, and lowered her toes to the carpet.

Steadying herself, she tottered slowly to the desk. As she sank into the chair, something on top of the pile of papers caught her eye.

A long, cream envelope, with URGENT stamped across it. An envelope she was certain she'd seen before.

Holding her breath she stretched out her hand until it was almost touching the envelope. She held it there, then snatched her fingers away as if the paper was on fire. She sat back for a few moments, regaining her breath. Digging her nails into her palms, she leaned forward until she could see the lettering on the envelope.

On the bottom left hand corner she read the words: *In case of non-delivery please return to: Alderney Private Hospital, 44 Creek Street . . .*

Suddenly the words blurred and the room began to tilt again and all she could think of was getting back to bed. As she staggered across the room she saw something else, that in one swift moment sucked all the breath from her lungs.

How had she not noticed it before? It must have been there on the bedside table all this time . . .

Clutching it to herself she fell back onto the bed and stroked its smooth shiny surface until her fingers found the spot where the one little tusk was missing.

★   ★   ★

'Do you feel up to talking now, Lisa?

'What about?' she asked, pretending to have been asleep and keeping her head down to hide her red eyes, thankful that she had heard the front door in time to replace the little ivory carving on the bedside table.

Guy sat down in the leather chair, facing his desk. He looked across at her, then down at the envelope she had so nearly touched.

'There's so much,' he said, shaking his head. 'I don't know where to start.'

'You must have been shattered when Iliana married Tony,' she said, for something to break the awkward silence, and also to settle a niggling doubt in her mind.

'Not really. Tony's always been crazy about her and she's just been playing hard to get. One day she'll be a fine composer. I wish I could have used her music instead of Orsino's, but — '

He stopped suddenly, his face creasing into a frown of confusion. 'Lisa? You don't think . . . oh no! You think there was something between Iliana and me! I was only trying to encourage her to keep composing music — '

'Your tent was close to mine. I couldn't help overhearing your conversation the day we returned from

Chilangola . . . '

Guy's face relaxed. 'Oh! You mean when I told her Orsino had finally signed the contract to write the music? That news was a bitter blow. I told her not to give up hope but to keep trying and I would keep helping her all I could.'

Lisa remembered Iliana telling her she would go anywhere to be near Guy. No wonder, she thought guiltily, if it gave her a chance to get her work recognised . . .

But suddenly she couldn't resist the temptation to ask him about Sally Lomas. After all these years, before she said her final goodbye, she had to know. She gripped the edges of the bed, hating herself for what she was about to say, but unable to stop herself.

'And I suppose there was nothing between you and Sally Lomas. You sure looked friendly the night before you went to South America.' She could still see Guy pressed against Sally's willowy body, the red hair shrouding them both.

Still feel the pain burning through her as she fled down the stairs.

'I think this malaria has gone to your head, Lisa Ryding,' he said gently. 'Why dredge up poor Sally? She had just lost her fiancé in a tragic motorbike accident . . . '

What was he saying? He was confusing her. 'You mean she wasn't — '

With two strides he was at the bedside, kneeling beside her so that his face was level with hers. 'Lisa, are you telling me that seeing me comforting Sally was the reason you walked out on me?'

'I didn't walk out on you. I left because to me it was plain I had misconstrued your friendship. And because — Oh, it doesn't matter any more. But you see . . . I thought . . . well . . . before that, you'd made me think that you and I . . . that we — '

'Lisa. Calm down. What are you trying to say?'

'Oh, I don't know how to say this . . . but . . . you'd made me think that you cared for me — '

'*Cared* for you? I *loved* you. I still do. I always have. But surely you *knew* that! Oh Lisa . . . '

For the next sixty seconds they stared at each other, neither one of them moving. On the outside Lisa felt as though her skin was on fire, while on the inside it seemed as if everything had frozen into one solid immovable block.

'Guy?' she whispered, wildly excited at what he was saying but still not really believing it was true. 'Don't you see? It was because I was so sure that you *didn't* love me that I left.'

'I don't believe this. You must have been aware of my feelings for you. Couldn't you have trusted me?'

'How could I when you were in another woman's arms?'

'I told you. That didn't mean *anything*. Why were you so suspicious?'

'You never *told* me you loved me — '

He gripped her arms. 'Lisa, I *couldn't* . . . '

'And when I saw you with Sally

Lomas I realised how foolish I'd been to imagine you had any special feelings for me — '

'Ah! So you *had* realised that I had special feelings for you. And you were so right. I did! I loved you. You have no idea what I went through — '

'Guy, you're talking in circles. You never even hinted — '

He slid his hand down her arm. 'No, Lisa. I didn't. Because I *couldn't* — ' He looked down, then quickly looked up again with a raw look in his eyes. 'I wanted to. But you were so young. In your first year. If I'd said anything about how I felt I'd never have been able to leave you — ' He squeezed his eyes closed as though he couldn't bear what he was saying. 'And that would have been . . . *impossible.*'

Couldn't? Impossible? What did he mean?

'You were afraid I was getting too serious and you didn't know how to tell me so you decided to make it obvious without words. Well, I got the message,

Guy. Loud and clear. There was no hope of any commitment from you. There would always be someone else — '

Guy took her hand in his. 'No, Lisa. You're not listening. You still don't understand. I knew nothing about the plans for that night. It was a surprise farewell party. They arrived out of the blue. Filled the fridge with drinks. Brought all that food. How could I say we didn't want them there? It would have been so unkind.

'I was waiting for you to arrive. I wanted you to mingle with the others for a short while until it was convenient to slip away, just the two of us. But when I found you'd gone I assumed you'd changed your mind about me. I was distraught. You see, there was something very important I was going to tell you before I went away . . . '

She stared at him blankly. 'I'm sorry. How was I supposed to know?'

'You were supposed to have more faith in me.'

'I'd never had faith in anyone. How was I to know that you were any different? Suddenly I was certain I'd only been someone to tag along with at the Photographic Society. You were going to Brazil and I was no longer needed. Whooping it up on your last night with all your sophisticated friends was clearly far more fun than spending a dreary evening with me — '

'Lisa you must know now that none of that is true. When I couldn't find you I went to your room but you'd already left. I looked everywhere. I even went to the station. There was no sign of you. Monica King knew nothing. Where *did* you go? And how did you manage to vanish so quickly?'

Lisa hardly dared look at him. 'I . . . I had my suitcase packed. I had my air ticket to Brazil. You see . . . I was going to go with you. It was going to be a surprise. The way you were always surprising me . . . '

He threw his head back and screwed

up his eyes. 'It would *not* have been *possible!*'

'It would have been very easy — '

'No Lisa. It wouldn't.'

She turned away, hating the finality of his words, feeling them eating into her like acid.

And in that moment she made up her mind. She would get up out of this bed and leave. Never see him again, but first she would tell him the truth.

'I was going to make love to you that night. So you'd have no choice but to take me with you,' she said boldly, surprised at how easily she'd been able to tell him.

'Oh, Lisa — ' He took several deep breaths. 'There was no *way* I'd have made love to you that night. Not that night or any other night — although I wanted to, more than anything else in the world. No, wait, look at me. Let me tell you because, you see, that night I was going to ask you to — '

'What?'

'To wait for me.'

'I don't understand. You mean — get engaged?'

'No! That would not have been possible.'

'Guy. You're talking in riddles.' Why did he keep saying that everything would have been impossible?

'Lisa. This may sound cruel to you even now. But I was only thinking of you. No, that's not true. I was selfish too. I didn't want to lose you. But you were still only a *girl*. You'd just left school. How could I let you throw a brilliant future to the winds? Of *course* I wanted you to come with me. It would have been wonderful. But I couldn't rob a promising young student of her career after only one year.'

'I didn't care. I wanted so badly to come with you that I'd have done anything.'

'Don't think I didn't know. Don't think I was blind to the way you felt about me. And don't think I wasn't tempted. I'd tried so hard not to be tempted. But I wanted you forever,

Lisa. Not just a year. And that wasn't possible. Not then and not in the foreseeable future. And even if it had been I would at least have waited until you'd graduated — '

He paused, and once more the look of pain crossed his face.

'You see. That night. I was going to tell you that *I* would wait for you — ' He put his hands on her arms. 'If *you* — would wait for me.'

Lisa stared at him. 'If *I* would wait . . . for *you!*'

He stood up and walked to the desk. Picked up the long cream envelope and started pacing up and down the room.

'When you disappeared I was devastated. I'd been a fool. I'd obviously been completely wrong about how you felt. I had lost you. You had clearly decided there was no future for us, otherwise you'd have contacted me.'

'I wouldn't have dreamt of it,' she answered, 'because I thought that you — '

She looked at Guy and frowned.

Then she smiled and slowly shook her head, her eyes widening because all of a sudden the jigsaw pieces were slotting into place and beginning to make sense.

Except for one thing.

She looked at the long cream envelope, still in his hand.

'Guy?'

'Yes?'

'There's something you're not telling me, isn't there?'

He nodded. 'Read this, Lisa.'

She clenched her fists.

'*Read it*,' he said.

She took the letter from him.

12

Lisa never knew who it was that had comforted whom.

In the half-hour that they lay locked in each other's arms, words had not been necessary. Closeness, and knowledge that nothing could ever keep them separated again, was all that was needed to heal the torment in their hearts.

'And to think that we so nearly walked out of each other's lives,' she mused, shaking her head as Guy finally looked at her, his tears barely dry.

'We *did* walk out of each other's lives, Lisa. We took it in turns! And all because I didn't communicate openly and honestly. When I think how hurt you must have been that night, and all I'd needed to do was make sure you knew what had happened — as soon as you arrived at the party. I'll never forgive myself for that lapse.'

He lowered his head. 'But especially for keeping you in the dark about my marriage to Anthea until it was too late. You see, that's what I was going to tell you that night — the night before I went to Brazil.'

Gently she lifted his chin and turned his face towards her. 'I was just as much to blame. I acted hastily. If I'd stopped to talk to anybody at the party, I'd have found out what was going on. Then I'd have stayed. And I'd have known about Anthea. And the baby. And I'd have understood everything.'

'Lisa Ryding, it's no wonder I fell in love with you when you were just eighteen. And knowing now how close I was to not having you will make me treasure you all the more.'

'Oh, Guy — '

He put his finger on her lips. 'No, don't say anything. I've tired you out enough. You're going to rest now and when you wake up I'll have a surprise for you. *Two* surprises!'

'You and your surprises.'

He kissed her, then drew the curtains and tiptoed out.

Lisa lay on the bed, her heart beating wildly, unable to close her eyes as she thought of the agony Guy had endured for eight long years.

★　★　★

It was already dark when she heard the doorbell ring. Who could that be, she wondered. Guy would have his key so it couldn't be him.

A few minutes later Guy came through the bedroom door and swept her into his arms.

'I hope you're hungry,' he said, ignoring her protests as he carried her to the dining room where a waiter was just taking a bottle of champagne out of a silver ice bucket before slipping discreetly away.

There were no lights on in the dining room. A single silver candelabra lit the room, casting a glow on Guy's hair that reminded her of the night when the only light was from the stars and the gibbous moon . . .

Ignoring the bemused look on Lisa's face, Guy helped her into a chair, straightening the striped pyjama top as though it was a priceless ball gown. With his fingers he delicately pushed the hair out of her eyes, then stood back and smiled.

'You look stunning!' he said.

Lisa couldn't help smiling too, but was still puzzled by the elaborate lengths Guy had gone to when a simple boiled egg would have been all she needed.

She watched him fill the champagne flutes.

'This *is* a surprise,' she said. 'But you said there were two. What's the second one?'

'Wait and see,' he said, handing her a glass. 'In fact, there are two more. But right now, let's drink to us.'

He clinked his glass against hers.

'To us,' she replied, hearing her voice but wondering if she was really awake, or if this was just one more of her vivid dreams.

Suddenly he put down his glass and reached into his pocket, never taking his eyes off Lisa's.

She held her breath, squinting at the small blue box in his hand, gasping as he removed the plain solitaire diamond from its bed of blue velvet.

Slowly he reached for her hand. 'I hope it fits,' he said, slipping it onto her finger.

Tears filled her eyes. 'It's beautiful! Oh, Guy, I didn't know I could be so happy.'

'Well, you won't be happy if you don't hurry up and eat that food. Nor will the caterers, who went to great lengths to find a perfect paw-paw, and boerewors made from exactly the same recipe you thought was so wonderful in the bush.'

Lisa had no idea that she was so hungry. Nor had she ever realised how evocative smells and tastes could be, the paw-paw and the boerewors taking her back to the raw beauty of the evergreen trees, the yellow grass, the vast open skies. The elephants.

'I can almost smell the wood smoke from the camp fire,' she said, as she finished the last morsel.

Guy looked at his watch. 'Come on, we're just in time.'

Paying no attention to the bewildered look on Lisa's face he picked her up once more and carried her into the lounge. He sat her down on the sofa, settled himself next to her and pressed the TV remote.

'Oh, look, Guy — 'The New Dawn!'

'Uh huh. I didn't think you'd want to miss it's first showing on TV.'

Lisa bit her bottom lip as the woodland scenes unfolded. Scenes that brought back to life the re-awakening of her love for Guy.

'Why did you call it 'The New Dawn?' she asked.

Guy pressed his lips together as though he was not sure of how to answer her.

At last he spoke. 'Because of the way you looked at me in the helicopter on the way to Lusaka.'

With her eyes still on the television screen Lisa saw his face superimposed in exactly the way she had seen it that morning in the glow of the African sunrise. When high above the wilderness her love for him had been intensified to the point where she knew that she could no longer fight it.

Guy squeezed his eyes into tight slits, then opened them and pressed the remote. As the picture disappeared Lisa turned to face him.

'Anthea had just died,' he said. 'For eight years I'd been consumed with guilt and sorrow and recriminations, but at that moment in the helicopter I suddenly realised that I couldn't spend the rest of my life looking back. At last it was time to let go.'

Lisa knew what he meant. Since her father had died she had finally come to terms with the knowledge that her sorrow and anger had to stop. That she couldn't go on blaming her father for her mother's death and for his inability to give his only daughter any affection whatsoever.

'After eight years my life was suddenly in front of me,' Guy said. 'You were pretending to look at the sunrise but I knew you were looking at me. And I knew what you were thinking. It still wasn't the moment to tell you, but I hoped that if I was patient — and if I was lucky — there was a chance that we'd meet again and that everything was going to work out. A new life — a new dawn — lay ahead . . . '

Lisa smiled through her tears. 'You always could read my mind, couldn't you, Guy? Except that in that instance I was convinced I'd never see you again!'

'Well, you were wrong,' Guy said, and pressed the remote again.

Although she'd already seen the preview, watching the scenes unfold while Guy held her in his arms brought them to life as it never had at the Soho studio.

'Oh, Guy, do you remember that?' she said, as the old matriarch lumbered at eye level into the full width of the screen, head high and trunk waving, trumpeting and shaking the earth as she charged feet first towards the camera.

When Guy remained silent Lisa took her eyes off the screen to look at him. Sensing her movement, he too turned away from the screen. 'You could have been killed taking those shots,' she whispered. 'I remember how terrified I was.'

'Terrified?' He touched her arm. 'Do you think I would have taken such a risk? When life had so much to offer?'

'How d'you mean?'

His finger traced the outline of her lips. 'I always hoped that one day we'd be together. I didn't care how long I had to wait.'

'I just wish you'd told me about Anthea and the baby right at the beginning, when we first met. How dreadful it must have been to keep that sorrow to yourself. I don't know how you managed it for eight long years. Not just the agony of losing your baby son, but losing your wife as well. Because if Anthea was in an irreversible coma all that time, she might as well have been dead.' She squeezed his hand, amazed at how simple it had become to speak openly and frankly.

Guy's jaw tightened. 'I fought with my conscience. Although love for you overwhelmed me, remorse filled my heart. I wanted to tell you. I almost did, but I always thought that I would be betraying Anthea's memory to tell people that she was alive, but that she was really dead. Then even when she finally died I was afraid to speak. As you well know — '

Lisa nodded, remembering clearly how distraught he'd been. 'It must have been terrible to know that all they had to do at any time was press a switch. Why didn't you let them do it sooner?' She held her cheek against his, wishing she had known of the torment he'd been enduring. 'Wouldn't it have been kinder?' she asked gently. 'Why eight years?'

Guy buried his face in her shoulder. 'Because it was my fault. If I hadn't neglected them, if I hadn't stayed in London for five days a week running that wretched law firm, leaving them alone in the country, Anthea wouldn't have been driving to the station to meet me on that terrible stormy Friday night. And the car would never have skidded out of control. Somehow, I had to keep her alive. The life support machine was the only way I knew how.'

She pulled him towards her and stroked his brow, feeling every stab of pain she knew he was still feeling.

'But I've learned my lesson, Lisa. Anthea has finally gone, bless her, but I won't ever leave you alone — '

Suddenly there was loud trumpeting from the elephants on the screen. Guy reached for the remote.

'No! Don't turn it down!' she said. 'I love to hear the sound they make. If it hadn't been for them . . . '

'Hush, my darling. I don't even want to think of the consequences.'

THE END

We do hope that you have enjoyed reading this large print book.

Did you know that all of our titles are available for purchase?

We publish a wide range of high quality large print books including:
Romances, Mysteries, Classics
General Fiction
Non Fiction and Westerns

Special interest titles available in large print are:
The Little Oxford Dictionary
Music Book, Song Book
Hymn Book, Service Book

Also available from us courtesy of Oxford University Press:
Young Readers' Dictionary
(large print edition)
Young Readers' Thesaurus
(large print edition)

For further information or a free brochure, please contact us at:
Ulverscroft Large Print Books Ltd.,
The Green, Bradgate Road, Anstey,
Leicester, LE7 7FU, England.
Tel: (00 44) **0116 236 4325**
Fax: (00 44) **0116 234 0205**